Home Sweet Haunted Home

by Jane Sorenson

illustrated by Kathleen L. Smith

D0681125

STANDARD PUBLISHING

Cincinnati, Ohio

24-02937

LIBRARY OF CONGRESS
Library of Congress Cataloging-in-Publication Data

Sorenson, Jane.
   Home sweet haunted home/by Jane Sorenson; illustrated
by Kathleen Smith.
      p. cm.–(A Katie Hooper book; 2)
   Summary: Katie and her new friend Sara have many ad-
ventures searching for treasure and a ghost in the old Victo-
rian house that is the Hooper family's new home.
   ISBN 0-87403-487-6
   [1. Moving, Household–Fiction. 2. Family life–
Fiction. 3. Christian life–Fiction.] I. Smith, Kathleen,
1950- ill. II. Title. III. Series: Sorenson, Jane. Katie
Hooper book; 2.
PZ7.S7214Ho 1988
[Fic]–dc19   88-6398
                                                   CIP
                                                    AC

The Adventure Begins

I sat in the back seat of Purple Jeep and tied my shoes. It wasn't easy, because our four-wheel-drive is so old it trembles—even on smooth highway.

In the front seat, Mom chattered non-stop. Dad mostly drove and listened.

Recently, Mom has been sleeping late in the mornings. Our baby is due in a few weeks, and Mom has trouble sleeping at night. But today, she was the first one up.

"I just can't wait to see the inside of the house!" Mom was saying.

That's where we're going—to see our new home. It's a huge old wreck of a house on land just south of Woodland Park, Colorado. We're getting to live there almost for free.

Jason, my older brother, sat in the back seat beside me. "It's still hard for me to believe we're moving," he said. "We've lived in that log cabin all my life."

"M. McDuff says we can visit whenever we want to," I reminded him. M. is a real-live author who just bought the cabin. We only rented it.

"Once we leave, the cabin won't be the same," Jason said. And in my heart I realized that probably he was right.

While I watched the sun light up the mountains, I listened to Mom. "It's a miracle, Steve," she told Dad. "All my life I've wanted to live in a Victorian house. I have a million ideas for fixing it up."

My brother turned to me. "I hope the inside is better than the outside," he said.

I was the only one who heard him. "Don't be so negative," I told him. "Can't you see how excited everybody is?"

"All I can think of is all the work," Jason said.

"Well," I admitted, "fixing up the house probably will be a lot of work, but we'll have fun doing it." My brother didn't say anything.

In the front seat, Mom kept bubbling. "When we first found out the cabin was being sold, I could hardly believe it," she said. "Still, I just knew God would provide a place for us to live."

"I was really depressed when I thought His choice was that raised ranch," Dad admitted. "After fifteen years of life on fifty acres, I couldn't picture us on a tiny lot in town."

"We would have managed," Mom said.

"Well, Elizabeth, the Lord has His ways," Dad said.

"It really is a miracle," Mom said again.

Woodland Park was just waking up when we drove into town. In August, the population is still mainly tourists, and they sleep late.

Dad found a parking place right in front of the bank. "Do you want to come in?" he asked.

"We'll wait for you, Steve," Mom said.

I watched my father climb down and walk across into the bank. For such a large man, he is very graceful. Today he was wearing a tan cowboy hat. Dad is afraid of horses, but the hat hides his bald spot.

Mom turned around in her seat. "You're awfully quiet back there."

I waited for Jason to say something, but he didn't. "I was thinking about Sara Wilcox," I said. "I can't wait to see her again."

"The Lord not only gave us a home, but He also gave you the friend you've been praying for," Mom said.

I grinned and thought of Sara's bright red

hair. "Well, Sara isn't exactly what I pictured in my mind," I admitted. "But the amazing thing is that *she* was praying for a friend, too!"

Mom smiled. "Maybe there'll be a friend for you, too, Jason."

"Right," my brother said. He didn't sound convinced.

Dad returned alone. He held up a key. "Harry Upjohn is tied up in a meeting, but we can go on over to the house. Everything's all set except for signing some papers."

"I can hardly wait," Mom said.

On the highway south of town, Dad missed the turn-off to the property, and we had to turn around. It didn't seem as far as when we were following Mr. Upjohn.

Then, suddenly, we were in front of the house. Dad parked by the road, and we just sat there and looked.

"Well, there it is," Dad said.

At first, even Mom was speechless.

There, in the middle of waist-high weeds, stood what is probably the ugliest house in the whole world. In the morning light it looked even worse than when Mr. Upjohn first showed it to us last week.

The banker had called it a wreck. He told Mom it was no place for a family, and now I wondered if he might have been right. It had stood vacant for more than a year, while the bank tried to sell the land around it. But nobody had bought the property.

"I guess if it were wonderful, somebody would have bought it," Dad said, finally. "And it isn't as if it costs a lot of money. We just have to pay taxes and insurance."

"It's funny," Mom said. "I was so sure it was yellow."

"I think it used to be white," Dad said.

It was hard to tell. On the first floor, the windows and door were all boarded up. Upstairs, a green curtain still flapped out through broken glass.

"What's the key for?" Jason asked. "It looks like what we need is a crowbar."

"It's for the back door," Dad said.

Fortunately, just at that point, Mom's excitement returned. "Hey," she reminded us, "don't forget, we're looking at an adventure here. You can't have an adventure if you never take a chance!"

"Elizabeth, you're incredible!" Dad glanced at her and smiled. Then he turned to Jason and me. "Your mom still sounds just like she did when we eloped!"

Mom pointed to the house and laughed. "I'd like to introduce Sleeping Beauty!"

"Just waiting to be kissed," I said.

"Oh, no," Jason groaned. But now even he was smiling.

"OK," Dad said, as he opened Purple Jeep's door, "Adventure, here we come! Let's have a look inside."

Dad helped Mom down from Purple Jeep. He never used to do that, but, to be honest, she is kind of clumsy right now.

"Follow me," Dad said, as he started off through the weeds. After several steps, he turned to warn us. "Be careful. Somebody must have used this property for a dump!" He reached down and held up an old ironing board.

"Ah, wilderness!" Mom laughed.

It took us a good ten minutes to make our way around to the back porch. While the rest of us stood there watching, Dad produced the key from his pocket.

Surprisingly, the lock turned. Then, as Dad pushed the door open, the rusty hinge squeaked twice. *Eeek!* and then *Eeeeeeeeeek!*

Personally, I wasn't surprised that the door squeaked. Somehow, I just knew it would. Isn't that how adventures always begin?

Home Sweet Yucky Home

The door swung halfway open and then stopped.

Mom giggled. "You'll have to open it farther than that, or I'll have to wait outside."

Dad pushed, but the door wouldn't budge. "I don't think I'll fit either," he said. "I guess Jason or Katie will have to go in and see what's in the way."

Frankly, I didn't expect to be a hero this soon. "You do it, Jason," I said.

We watched my brother disappear into the opening. In a few seconds, he was back. "I need a flashlight," he said.

"There's one in Purple Jeep," Dad said. "I'll get it." He trotted off.

"What's it like?" Mom asked Jason.

"It's so dark I can't really tell," he said. "There's something heavy in front of the door."

"Is it scary in there?" I asked.

"Scary?" Jason took a deep breath. "Are you kidding?"

Well, I wasn't kidding, but I couldn't admit it. At least not while my brother was acting so macho.

"Here you are," Dad said, smiling. He had taken off his cowboy hat, and his hair curled at the temples.

Jason took the flashlight and disappeared again. But this time, he stayed longer. Finally, Dad called, "Jason, just check the door. We want to come in, too."

Jason, covered with dust and brushing spider webs out of his eyes, returned. "It's the stove," he said. "The stove is in front of the door. Somebody must have wanted to keep people out."

"Is it a big one?" Dad asked.

"I don't know," Jason said. "Big enough, I guess."

"Can you pull on it while the rest of us push on the door?" Dad wondered.

"I'll try. Say when."

There wasn't really room for all three of us to push, but we tried to take our places in front of the door. "OK," Dad said, "push."

12

Nothing happened.

"Let's try it again," Jason called. "I wasn't ready."

"One, two, three, push." Slowly the door opened several more inches. Now there was room for Dad to squeeze in. And several minutes later all the Hoopers stood bunched together in the kitchen.

It took a few minutes for my eyes to adjust to the darkness. Jason kept flashing his light around from one place to the next.

And then Mom started to laugh. This was no puny giggle. It was one of those contagious laughs that just wouldn't stop. Naturally, the rest of us joined in. Soon tears were running down my face, and I felt weak.

"Oh, my," Mom said, finally. "Home Sweet Home."

"It will be a while before you can put up wallpaper, Elizabeth," Dad said.

"I'll have to settle for being able to fix a meal," Mom admitted. "Don't tell me there's no sink!"

"I think I see sink legs hanging out underneath those newspapers," Dad said.

Standing there in such chaos, I suddenly was filled with appreciation for my mother. There Mom stood, shaped like an upside-down light bulb, laughing her head off. If she had cried, who knows what would have happened next!

"Let's try the next room," Mom suggested. "It couldn't be any worse."

Well, she was wrong. Of course, I must admit that the Hoopers are hardly the neatest family alive! To be honest, we didn't even know our cabin was being sold because we lost that day's mail on the messy coffee table! But this was different.

I mean, there's good mess, and there's bad mess. And this was definitely bad. Old newspapers, broken-down furniture, dirty dishes, empty cans, filthy clothing, cardboard boxes, rusty pans. Well, you get the idea. And someone had painted the walls in the second room black.

"Flash the light over here, Jason," Dad said.

Mom and I watched.

"What do you see, Dad?" my brother asked.

"I just realized that there's a path through this room. Somebody must have gone through here," Dad said.

"As a matter of fact, there had to be a path through the kitchen, too," Mom said. "I mean, once we moved the stove, we didn't have to move anything else."

"So," I said, "what does that mean? Is somebody staying here, or what?"

"I don't see how anybody could be here now," Dad said. "But I suppose the house could have been used by someone in the past."

"It gives me the creeps to think about it," Mom said.

Altogether, in addition to the kitchen, there were three more rooms on the first floor. Because the windows were all boarded up, it was hard to see.

We didn't even try to walk into the last two rooms. Located on both sides of the stairway, they were both full of trash. Since they didn't lead anywhere, they had no passageways through them at all.

In the hall, Dad opened a narrow door. "Be careful, Katie! Don't fall. That must be the cellar!"

It looked pitch black. And, since my brother had the flashlight, I couldn't see to look down. All at once I felt cold, and I started to shiver.

"I'll bet there's water down there," Dad said. "It sure smells damp."

Oddly, considering how messy everything else was, the stairs going up to the second floor were clear. And the stairway itself was beautiful.

Mom noticed it, too. "What a remarkable banister," she said. "Look, it's never even been painted!" She started to smile. "At last I have something that's nice to start with. I wonder if I'll ever get the rest of the place to look as pretty as the stairway!"

Upstairs, Dad opened a door in the hall and

closed it again. "It's a bathroom. Don't look in, Elizabeth," he warned. "It will make you sick!" I didn't look either.

We found four large bedrooms. Since the windows up here weren't boarded up, there was more light, and it was easier for us to see. We no longer had to stay so close together.

In a front bedroom, I saw the ugly green curtain flapping through the broken window. But when I tried to pull it inside, the curtain fell apart in my hand.

With four bedrooms, each Hooper kid would have his own room—even the baby! I tried to picture how my stuff would look in one of the rooms, but I really couldn't.

"Look," Dad called, "there's another stairway. We have a third floor."

It was up there that I found my favorite spot. A tiny tower room with a circle of windows! Oh, if only I could claim this place for my own! Please, Lord!

I rubbed the corner of a window, and my finger turned black. But now I could even see Purple Jeep. And there, looking up at me, was my new friend, Sara Wilcox. Even from way up here, you couldn't miss that red hair! I waved. She didn't move. Probably she couldn't see me.

"Katie," Mom called. "Oh, there you are! We thought you had disappeared!"

"Isn't this room great!" I said. "And look, Mom! I can see Sara standing down there."

"Well, Katie, for goodness sake. You've discovered a turret!" Mom said. She smiled. "Want to know something? I always dreamed of having a turret when I was a girl."

"Do you think it could be mine?" I asked. "Please?"

Mom, still smiling, came over and hugged me. "I think it could be arranged," she said. "I guess maybe every girl dreams of having a little tower room. At this point, you're the only girl the Hoopers have."

Suddenly, my eyes filled with tears. "This place really is going to turn into a home, isn't it?"

"Of course it is," Mom said. "The yucky mess is just temporary. You just need faith to look beyond what you can see with your eyes."

"It will be our Home Sweet Home," I said. "I can see it—almost."

On the way out, I turned for a final glance at my little turret. And then I smiled. I realized I was feeling happier than I had in weeks.

Hidden Surprises

Mom and I started downstairs. When we reached the first floor hall, she stopped. "Katie, we're just about finished in the house for now. Why don't you go out and talk to Sara? We'll be out in a few minutes."

Just then we heard a crash, followed by silence.

"Steve! Jason! Are you OK?" Mom called.

"Don't yell, Elizabeth," Dad said. "I'm in the next room."

"What happened?" Mom asked. "Are you hurt?"

"I'll be OK," Dad said. "I tripped. I guess I can't manage without the flashlight after all."

"Speaking of the flashlight, where is Jason?"

Mom asked. Personally, I had no idea, and Dad didn't say anything either. "Jason," Mom called.

Silence.

"Jason," Dad called. "Where are you?" I could just make out Dad's shape as he stood up between the boxes.

"Now where could he be?" Mom wondered.

"When was the last time you saw him?" Dad asked.

"He was in one of the back bedrooms," I said. "Do you want me to go up and look?"

But before Dad could answer, my brother called down from upstairs. "Hey, you'll never guess what I found!"

"We thought you had gone outside," Mom said. "Didn't you hear us call?"

"Nope," Jason said. "I'll be right down." He came running down the stairs. "Guess what? I discovered a secret passage!"

"Where?" I asked.

"If I told you, it wouldn't be a secret anymore," Jason said.

"Can he do that?" I asked.

"I guess he can," Mom said.

But Jason was too excited to keep his discovery secret for long. "It starts from a closet in one of the bedrooms," he said.

"And where does it go?" Dad asked.

"That's the funny part," Jason said. "It goes so

far, and then it just stops."

"When we come back to the house, you can show us," Mom said. "For now, we'd like you to lead us back through the kitchen."

"My pleasure!" Jason said. Now he was smiling.

"Well, Elizabeth, what do you think?" Dad asked, as he locked the back door. "Do you see the possibilities?"

"I do," Mom grinned. "Of course, you have to look past the trash. But once we get the place cleared out, I don't see too many other problems. Do you?"

"I'd better see about having a dumpster brought out here," Dad said. "We'll need a place to put the junk."

"But can you clean the place out by yourself?" Mom asked. "Frankly, I can't see Katie and me being much help. And Jason still has his commitment at the sheep ranch."

"I'll help," I protested.

Jason interrupted. "I'm sure the Cochrans will understand if Dad needs me," he said. "I've already finished my summer projects. To be honest, I think they're just trying to keep me busy until school starts."

"That's great, Jason!" Dad said. "I really was hoping you could help me. I guess we could probably use another person, also," Dad admitted.

"We don't have forever." He looked at Mom. "The baby could come at any time."

Mom nodded. "Maybe Harry Upjohn knows someone who could help us," she suggested. "We could ask when we stop at the bank to sign the papers."

"A great idea," Dad said.

"Katie wants to see her new friend," Mom remembered. "Go on ahead, Katie. We're going to look at the yard. We'll be along in a minute."

I ran through the path we had made in the weeds.

Sara stood and watched me. When I reached her, she didn't even say hello. "Did you find it?" she asked.

"I don't know what you're talking about," I said.

"You don't?" Sara asked.

"Of course not," I said. "Did you see me wave to you from the turret?"

"I don't even know what a turret is," Sara said.

"You don't?" I asked.

"I don't even know what we're talking about," Sara said. "Are your conversations always like this?"

"Of course not," I said. "Are you saying it's my fault?"

"Well, I wasn't confused before you came." Sara grinned.

I grinned back. "How about if we try it again?" I suggested. "Let's pretend you don't even know I'm here."

"OK."

I ran back toward the house. After a few minutes, I turned around. I walked slowly toward Sara. "Hi, Sara," I said sweetly. "What a nice surprise to find you here this morning!"

"I'm kind of surprised myself," Sara said.

"You're supposed to say hello," I told her.

"Hello, Katie Hooper," Sara said. "How's my new neighbor this morning?"

"Fine," I said, "just fine. And how are you?"

"I'm fine, too," Sara giggled.

"See that little tower at the corner of the house?" I pointed. "On the third floor?"

"I see it," Sara said.

"To be honest, I just discovered it myself a little while ago," I told her. "My mother says every girl dreams of having a turret."

"I never did," Sara said. "Particularly since I never heard the word before."

"It's a tiny round room, like a tower on a castle," I explained. "It's cozy and special. Mom says it can be my special place."

"What will you do there?" Sara asked.

I thought a minute. "I'll think of something," I said. "Maybe you can even help me think of something."

"Maybe," Sara replied.

"Sara, I forgot what you asked me before," I said.

"Oh," Sara remembered. "I just wondered if you found it. Or maybe somebody in your family did?"

Suddenly, I thought of Jason's secret passageway. I wondered how Sara knew about it.

"Well, did you find it?" she asked again.

"Just exactly what do you think we might have found?" I asked.

"I'm talking about the secret treasure," Sara said. "Everybody around here thinks there's a secret treasure hidden inside that old house."

"No kidding!" I said. "Well, we didn't find it yet. But now that we know about it, we can start looking!" I grinned.

"I shouldn't have told you," Sara said.

"Of course you should have," I said. "After all, in order to find the treasure, a person would have to be able to get into the house. And we're the only ones with a key."

"I never thought of that," Sara said. She looked up. "Oh, here comes your father. I'd better split!" She started to run.

"No, Sara. Don't go," I called. "Stay and meet my family!" But by then she was running down the road.

Back at the Cabin

It was way past lunch time when Dad and Mom finished signing the papers giving us the right to fix up and live in Home Sweet Home. Although we were hungry, nobody said so. Dad pointed Purple Jeep toward our cabin.

The Hoopers almost never eat in a restaurant. Mom's idea of "fast food" is having everybody make his own sandwich. Until I went to school, I thought McDonald's was just the name of an old farmer!

"I hope January's OK," I said. To be honest, all morning I had forgotten about my dog. Dad was right, though. He would have been in the way.

"We'll have to rig up some way to tie him to a tree out at the new place," Dad said. "I guess I really don't trust him."

"January's never done any harm," Mom said. Dad didn't say anything.

When we first entered the cabin, we didn't see the dog. But then Mom called us into her and Dad's bedroom. "Look!" she said. "January's listening to the radio!"

What January is best at is making us laugh. And now we all had another good chuckle. Mom's clock-radio had come on, and January was sitting next to the bed with his head cocked.

"He might be dumb, but he has good taste," Dad said. "It's Mozart."

"Who's he?" Jason asked. Dad just looked at him.

"OK, everybody," Mom said. "Make your own sandwiches. I'll pour the milk."

After lunch, we all stayed around the table talking.

My brother looked discouraged. "I just don't see how we're going to get the house ready in time," Jason said. "I mean, what if the baby decides to come tonight?"

"We have to trust God's timing," Mom said. "It's like trusting Him for anything else."

"But the job is overwhelming," Jason said. "Even with the dumpster coming tomorrow."

"Everything in life is overwhelming," Dad said. "What if you started worrying about all

the things you have to learn in eighth grade?"

"I guess I'd feel overwhelmed," Jason said.

"But if you go to school every day and keep up with your homework, you'll find it's no harder than seventh grade was!" Dad assured him.

Jason grinned. "Sometimes *thinking* about it is worse than actually *doing* it!"

"Exactly," Dad said. "Much of life is like that. We just have to face one day at a time. And then we can handle it."

"But what about help?" Jason asked. "Mr. Upjohn couldn't give us a single name of someone to help us."

"God knows what we need," Mom said. "If we need another worker, the Lord will provide one."

"I don't see how you can have so much faith," Jason said.

"They've had a lot of practice," I said. Everybody laughed. But I think it's true. I mean, when your father spends his life painting pictures of mountains, the whole family gets a lot of practice!

The telephone rang. Jason answered it and began to talk. "Oh, hi, Mr. Cochran!" he said. "I was going to call you. We just got home from going through the house.... It's going to be fine. Of course, it will be a lot of work. But we think Dad and I can handle it. That's what I was going to call about."

Mom stopped listening and turned to Dad. "I guess I'll have to get organized on this end," she said.

"I don't want you to overdo," Dad told her. "Maybe Katie can help you here. And, don't forget, Mayblossom McDuff isn't in a rush to move into the cabin."

"I know," Mom said. "She's wonderful about it. But it would be nice if we could move before Jason and Katie start school."

My brother hung up the phone and turned around. "I can't explain it," he said. "But when I was talking to Mr. Cochran, I just *knew* things would work out!"

Mom smiled at him. "It's called faith," she said.

After Dad made a few suggestions, Mom told him she'd get organized by herself. So Dad drove off to paint a mountain. Recently, he's been so involved in finding a place to live that he hasn't had much time to paint.

Jason washed the lunch and breakfast dishes, and I dried. Then he rode off on his bike for Cochrans'.

I took January outside. First, we both ran to the pines and back. Then I tried to teach him to obey, but I didn't know where to begin. Whenever I looked at him, it almost seemed as if he were laughing at me.

I was just about to give up and go in to talk to

Mom when a pickup turned into our lane. I don't think I had ever seen it before. A smiling woman greeted me. "I'm Penny Cochran," she said. "Is your mother home?"

"I'll get her," I said.

"I'm Elizabeth Hooper," Mom said, "Jason's mother."

"I kind of figured you were," Mrs. Cochran smiled. "I can't believe we've never met before."

"This is Katie, Jason's sister," Mom said. "Would you like to sit down?"

"Hi," Mrs. Cochran said. "Don't go away, Katie. I just stopped by to see how I can help your mother."

Mom seemed surprised. "I guess you've heard we're moving."

"As if you didn't have enough on your mind," Mrs. Cochran said. "How are you feeling?"

"I feel fine," Mom told her. "A little tired, and kind of clumsy, but fine."

Mrs. Cochran laughed. "How well I remember! I thought you might need some cartons for packing. We saved our boxes after our last move. If you can use them, they're yours!"

"That would be wonderful," Mom said. "I could start packing a few boxes a day."

"I'd like to help you," Mrs Cochran said.

Mom seemed embarrassed. "I think if I just had the boxes . . ."

"It's up to you. See how it goes. But I can usually spare an hour after lunch," Mrs. Cochran said. "And now I'm going to insist on something else. In case your husband isn't here, I want to take you to the hospital!"

"Now that's an offer I can't refuse!" Mom smiled. "To be honest, I've been wondering what I'd do if the baby comes while Steve's working in Woodland Park! The only solution seemed to be to ride down with him every day."

"Go only when you want to," Mrs. Cochran said. "I'll keep gas in the truck. Hope you wouldn't mind riding down the mountain in a pickup."

Mom laughed. "You've never seen Purple Jeep! Anything else will be an improvement."

"Count on me!" Mrs. Cochran stood up. "I have to get back. Here's my phone number!" She handed Mom a piece of paper.

"I'll put it next to the telephone," Mom said. "How can I thank you?"

"Just have another baby as nice as your first two!" Mrs. Cochran said. She smiled at me. "I'll have my husband bring you the cartons."

"What a nice lady," I said.

"I only wish I had met her sooner," Mom said. "I guess now and then I felt like you did, Katie. I got lonesome for a friend."

"Is it too late?" I asked. "I mean, could you still

be friends with Mrs. Cochran?"

Mom looked at me. "You're right!" she said. "We won't be living that far away!"

By evening Mom had the cartons. She packed her first one full of cleaning supplies to take to Woodland Park. She filled the second carton and marked it *Baby Things*. I watched while she put that one in the corner of her bedroom.

It wasn't long before I climbed the ladder to my bedroom in the loft. All at the same time, I was tired and excited. I just can't wait for all the wonderful things that are going to happen to the Hoopers!

An Ambitious Stranger

Mom must have been exhausted. She didn't even wake up when January walked backwards into the coffee table and knocked a plant on the floor. Well, actually, the accident was caused by the dog's tail.

Now Dad and I were crawling around trying to pick up the dirt with our fingers.

"That settles it," Dad said. "We'll have to take January along. It isn't fair to leave him here with your mother."

I don't really think January was smart enough to plan the whole thing. Anyhow, now he waited in the back seat of Purple Jeep with his tongue hanging out. Once we started off for Woodland Park, he thumped his tail twice and went to sleep. As usual.

"Will we need more than one wheelbarrow?" Jason asked Dad. I listened to my brother who was sitting in the front seat. His voice sounded lower than it did yesterday.

"I don't think so," Dad said. "If they put the dumpster next to the house, we can just throw a lot of the junk right out the windows!"

"I can't wait to get started," Jason said. I couldn't believe it. My brother sounded almost like a *man!*

Today, we drove right through town and turned at the correct place. And there was Home Sweet Home, ugly as ever. Only today there was a huge green dumpster parked right next to the house.

"All right!" Dad said. "Just where we wanted it! Let's go!"

All the noise woke January up. I had to think fast. "You can be the guard," I told him. "You can stay next to the dumpster in case anyone tries to steal something." My voice sounded like Mom's. She thinks people like a challenge.

And the funny thing is that January did rise to the occasion. He acted as if guarding that dumpster were the most important thing in the world! In fact, he sat there and guarded it all morning.

Dad and Jason pried the boards off the kitchen

windows, and we started a junk pile on the side porch. Dad opened the gate in the rear of the dumpster, but it saved time to throw things in from a window or the porch.

A broken chair was the first piece of junk to land in the dumpster. Dad and Jason cheered. And from then on, when something big got tossed away, everybody cheered.

Dad had said if I came along, I'd have to work. He put me in charge of small junk in the kitchen. And there was plenty of it—broken dishes, paper, rags, cans, bottles, boxes.

Once, when Dad walked past, he realized how much time I was spending running back and forth to the porch. "What you need, Katie, are some large trash bags. I'll put them on my list."

While I worked, I wondered where Sara was. I smiled. If Sara thought we were looking for the treasure, maybe she'd help me! But all morning she never showed up.

I decided that no one would hide treasure in a kitchen! But *why not?* Where *did* treasure get hidden? I tried to think. In a cave. In a ship sunk at the bottom of an ocean. Maybe in a book or in a secret desk drawer. I've never heard of treasure hidden in a rusty coffee pot!

But, just in case, I started looking inside of things. It didn't take much longer. In fact, I started getting excited, and that made me work

34

faster! By the time we had lunch, I could see an ever-expanding filthy kitchen floor!

"You're doing great!" Jason told me. "This is more fun than I expected!"

"Maybe sometime I'll tell you a secret about this house," I said. "It's something I heard from Sara Wilcox."

"Who's Sara Wilcox?" Jason asked.

"She's my new friend. You'll meet her sooner or later," I told him.

"Not sooner," Jason said. "We're going to eat and then go to town."

Dad spread our picnic lunch under a tree near where January waited. "The dog's been perfect," Dad said. "It's amazing!"

"Everyone needs responsibility," I reported. "January's guarding the dumpster!"

Dad laughed his head off. But later, when we got ready to do our errands, he scoffed at the idea of leaving January to guard the place while we were gone. "Let's not push our luck!" he said.

Before we left, Dad closed the back of the dumpster and locked the kitchen door. Then all of us, including January, headed off for Woodland Park.

"We're sure off to a good start!" Jason said.

"You're right," Dad agreed. "And Katie will have that kitchen cleared out in time for supper!"

I laughed.

With January asleep in Purple Jeep, we parked and went into the hardware store. I had been in before, with Mom, but Dad and Mr. Snyder didn't know each other.

"You a tourist?" Mr. Snyder asked.

"I'm Steve Hooper," Dad said. "We're fixing up an old Victorian house south of town."

"Not the Spook House?" Mr. Snyder asked.

"I never heard that name," Dad said. "It's property owned by the bank. Used to belong to somebody named Willard."

"That's the Spook House, all right," Mr. Snyder said.

"Why is it called that?" Dad asked.

"You got all day?" Mr. Snyder replied. "There's a million stories told about that house!"

"Mr. Snyder," I said, "remember me? I'm Katie Hooper. I was wondering. Have you ever heard about secret treasure in the house?"

"You bet!" Mr. Snyder said. "There's always been talk about treasure. Even back when I was a boy!" He laughed. "Ain't no secret!"

"I call it Home Sweet Home," I said. "Spook House isn't a good name for a place where a family's going to live!"

"Call the house what you want," Mr. Snyder said. "I doubt you gonna change what *other* folks call it!"

Dad took out his list. Mr. Snyder had everything in stock except window locks. But he said he'd order them.

"You need somebody to help you?" he asked.

Jason and I looked at each other.

"As a matter of fact, I could use somebody," Dad said.

"Funny thing," Mr. Snyder said. "There was a boy here this morning asking about work. Never saw him before. Tourists don't usually want to work!" He chuckled.

"How can I find him?" Dad asked.

"Don't rightly know," Mr. Snyder said. "If he comes back, want me to tell him you might have something?"

Dad nodded and took out a piece of paper. "He could call me tonight. We don't have a telephone down here yet."

"Spooks don't need telephones," Mr. Snyder said. He winked at me. "They use vibes!"

"Don't try to scare Katie," Dad said. "That isn't funny."

Mr. Snyder laughed. "Just kidding," he said. He laughed again.

We finished loading everything into Purple Jeep and were getting ready to leave when Mr. Snyder called out the door. "That's him," he pointed. "There's your helper."

We looked across the street. A tall young man

in jeans and a white tee shirt was walking slowly. He was eating an ice cream cone.

"Want me to go over and talk to him?" Jason asked.

Dad thought a second. "Sure," he said. "Why not?"

Dad and I watched while the two boys talked. Actually, Jason was doing most of the talking. The other boy was eating his ice cream. Then Jason pointed over at Purple Jeep. I felt stupid sitting there.

As the boys walked across to where we were waiting, January started growling. Oh, no! I hoped he wasn't going into his "Star Spangled Banner" routine—the one where he howls at the top of his lungs.

"Easy, Boy." The stranger talked softly, and January shut up.

"Dad," Jason said. "This is Robert Denver."

Dad put out his hand. "Pleased to meet you, Robert. May I call you Bob?"

"Sorry, Sir," Robert said. "I've never been called Bob. But I'm glad to meet you! Jason here says you might be needing some help."

"We're fixing up an old house," Dad said. "Does that interest you?"

"Yes, Sir!" Robert said. "It's exactly the sort of thing I had in mind!"

Robert Joins
the Crew

"I've spent some time around old houses," Robert said. "And I'm a hard worker. I think you'll be surprised, Mr. Hooper."

"I believe you, Robert," Dad said. "The problem is, I can't afford to pay you much."

Robert smiled. "You've probably already guessed. I'm too young to get a regular job."

"How old are you?" Jason asked.

"I'm nearly fifteen," he said. "Frankly, Sir, it isn't really money that I'm looking for. I was hoping to find something to do during the day."

"Do you live around here?" Dad asked.

"I'm from north of Denver," Robert said. "I'm just visiting here. Do you folks live in Woodland Park?"

"We live up near the Divide," Dad said. "But we'll be moving into the old house as soon as we get it fixed up. It's just south of town."

"Our cabin was sold to an author," I told him. "Her name is Mayblossom McDuff. Have you heard of her?"

Robert shook his head. "I don't think so."

"Do you want to ride back with us and see the house?" Dad asked.

"Yes, Sir!" Robert said. I couldn't believe how excited he was.

"You can sit back here with January and me," I offered.

"Katie, let the boys have the back seat," Dad said. "You come up here with me."

I felt kind of left out. Dad and I didn't talk. Meanwhile, the boys were having a fabulous time. I don't think I've ever heard my brother talk so much.

Come to think of it, I've never been around Jason's friends. Well, the truth is, my brother and I have never exactly *had* friends. I mean, our cabin really is in the boondocks!

Dad pulled up in front of Home Sweet Home. To be honest, I could see why people might call it Spook House!

"It's an elegant old mansion!" Robert said. "Just look at that gingerbread!"

"What gingerbread?" I asked. "I don't see any."

Robert laughed. "That's what you call all that fancy trim," he said. "See the railings and the cut-out places and the arches and stuff!"

Dad laughed, too. "Robert, until now we've been thinking mostly about features like broken windows!"

"I understand, Sir," Robert said.

"I'll show him around," Jason said. The boys ran toward the house.

"Hey, I need help carrying this stuff," Dad said. But the boys were out of sight.

"I'll do it," I offered.

January woke up and trotted beside me to his place next to the dumpster. Even the dog had a friend. A big green one!

"I'll get the door," Dad said. But by the time we reached the back porch, Jason and Robert were already inside.

"Surprise!" Jason hollered out a bedroom window.

"What in the world!" I said. "How did they get in?"

"They must have climbed in a window," Dad said. He turned the key, and I followed him in.

Soon the boys were back. Their eyes looked excited, and they were out of breath.

"It's a wonderful house," Robert said. "I'd really enjoy helping you fix it up."

"All right. It's settled then," Dad said. "And

Jason, don't forget—I'm in charge here."

"I'm sorry, Dad," Jason said. "What do you want us to do first?"

"The two of you should be able to pitch most of the stuff from upstairs right down into the dumpster," Dad said.

"Out the window?" Robert asked.

"That's right," Dad said. "Just be careful."

"We will," Jason promised. The boys looked at each other and smiled.

"Do you want me to keep working in the kitchen?" I asked. It sounded like a boring afternoon. Even with the large plastic trash bags to make the job easier.

"Want me to help you?" Dad asked. "Wouldn't your mother be encouraged if we could get all of this trash out of the kitchen!"

"We could be Trash Busters!" I said.

Dad grabbed a broom and started marching. "No more junk allowed in the Hooper kitchen!" he hollered.

"Home Sweet Clean Home!" I yelled.

And, just like that, I started having fun again! Dad and I laughed at everything. I even forgot about looking for the treasure.

While Dad and I worked, we could hear stuff being dragged across the floor upstairs. Soon one of the boys would yell, "Watch out below!" Then something would crash into the dumpster.

And Jason and Robert would cheer. It made me smile every time.

I filled one huge black trash bag with cans. "Who do you think left the house in such a mess?" I asked my father.

"Tramps, probably," Dad said. "Somebody who had no other place to stay. This hasn't been a private home for many years. Harry Upjohn said the house used to be a favorite spot for hippies."

"Tell me about hippies," I said. "Were you alive when there were hippies?"

Dad laughed. "Yes, I was alive then. In fact, Katie, some people thought I was one!"

"They thought you were a hippy!" I laughed. "No kidding! Were you one?"

"Not exactly," Dad said. "Oh, I wore old clothes and let my hair grow. Nearly all the kids did then."

"You had long hair!" I said. "No offense, but I can't imagine you with long hair!"

"I know," Dad laughed. "I could use some of it now!" He rubbed a hand over his balding head. "But I wasn't a radical. My friends and I didn't riot or do drugs or anything like that."

"Why did hippies do those things?" I asked.

Dad had stopped working. "Oh, some young people really were protesting things—like materialism and the Vietnam War. But I think a lot

44

of us just used the war as an excuse to rebel."

"You must have looked like a hippy," I said. "Is that why Mom's parents didn't want you and Mom to get married?" I had never really figured it out.

"That might have been part of it," Dad said. "Lots of parents and kids had trouble understanding each other."

Suddenly, through the open window we heard January howl. *AaaOooooooo! AaaOooooooo!* It was what I call his "Star Spangled Banner" routine. Usually he only does it whenever he sees Mayblossom McDuff.

"Oh, no!" I said. "Do you think M. has come to visit us?"

"I doubt it," Dad said. "You'd better quiet January down, or we'll have the entire neighborhood checking us out."

Well, it wasn't the entire neighborhood. It was just Sara Wilcox. She stood with her hands on her hips looking at the dumpster.

AaaOoooooooo! AaaOooooooo! And January sat there—with his nose in the air—and howled.

Sara Visits the Tower

"Can't you make that dog shut up?" Sara yelled. I couldn't tell if she was mad or scared. Maybe a little of both.

AaaOoooooooo! AaaOoooooooo!

I stood there. I didn't really know what to do.

AaaOoooooooo! AaaOoooooooo!

"What's wrong with that dog?" Sara called. With her red hair sticking up straight, she looked like a small rooster.

"Nothing's wrong with that dog," I hollered. "He's guarding the dumpster. What did you do?"

"Are you blaming me?" Sara yelled. "Give me a break!"

AaaOoooooooo!

I couldn't stand it any longer. "January," I

said, in my loudest and firmest voice, "be still!"

The dog closed his mouth. Slowly, he lowered his nose until his head hung low. He just looked at me.

"Wow!" Sara said. "Does he always obey like that?"

"I don't know. I never tried it before."

Although January had stopped howling, Sara stayed where she was. But she took her hands off her hips.

"I'm sorry," I said. "He usually only does that when he sees Mayblossom McDuff."

"Wrong," Sara said. "He did the same thing the last time he saw me. Don't you remember?"

She was right. It was the night we first saw the house. When Sara came over, I was sitting in Purple Jeep babysitting my dog. And when he saw her, January had howled then, too.

"It's a mystery," I said.

Sara started walking toward the porch, one step at a time. "Who's Mayblossom?"

"She bought our cabin," I explained.

"Oh. Maybe your dog thinks I look like her."

I laughed. "She's an older woman, sort of like a grandmother. She writes books."

Sara groaned. "I hate books."

I just looked at her. "You do?" I didn't know there were people who didn't like books. "What do you do for fun?"

"I watch television. Wanta know what my favorite programs are?"

"I wouldn't recognize them," I told her. "We don't have a TV."

"It's broken?"

"No, we've never had one."

Sara stood and looked at me. "You don't have a television? I never in my entire life met a person who didn't have a TV!"

"Well, you have now!"

We just stood and looked at each other.

Then my father stepped out onto the porch. "Hi! Is this the person who was trying to steal our trash?"

"I was not!" Sara looked as if she might run away again.

"Hey," Dad said softly, "I was just kidding."

"My dad's a big tease," I said. I turned to my father. "This is my friend, Sara Wilcox. And Sara, this is my father."

"Hi, Mr. Hooper," she said shyly.

"Hi, Sara. You live around here?" Dad asked.

She nodded and started to point.

Suddenly, from the upstairs window, Jason yelled. "Bombs away!"

And then Robert counted. "One, two, three . . ."

The crash into the dumpster scared even me.

"Yeahhhh!" cheered the boys.

Sara looked scared to death. "My mother told

48

me to stay away from here. She said there has to be a reason."

"A reason for what?" I asked.

"A reason it's called Spook House."

"They aren't spooks," I said. "That's just my brother Jason and Robert."

"It isn't usually this exciting around here," Dad laughed.

"Can Sara come in?" I asked.

Dad nodded. "She might get dirty."

I realized how different the kitchen looked. While I was outside talking to Sara, Dad had almost finished clearing out the rest of the trash. Of course, the room still looked filthy.

"Well," I giggled, "as you can probably tell, this is the kitchen. I've been working in here all day."

Sara didn't say anything.

"Well, you should have seen it before!"

Dad excused himself. "I'm going to get the boys to help me move the stove. See you soon."

Sara glanced all around. "I don't suppose you found it?" she asked.

"No, but I looked," I said.

"I never heard of a secret treasure hidden in a kitchen," Sara said.

"Me either, but you never can tell."

"Maybe the boys found it upstairs," Sara said.

"I doubt it," I said. "They probably aren't even

49

looking. My brother didn't pay any attention when Mr. Snyder and I were talking about it."

"Who's Mr. Snyder?" Sara asked. "Are you telling the whole world about it?"

"Of course not. He's just the man in the hardware store. He seemed to know a lot about a secret treasure," I said.

"Some secret!" Sara said. "How about that other guy upstairs?"

"Robert's from Denver. He wouldn't know about it."

Sara lowered her voice. "All the same, it wouldn't hurt to keep an eye on those guys!"

I nodded. I thought I heard footsteps. "I won't even mention the treasure."

Sara grinned. "I thought you'd never catch on."

Jason, Robert, and Dad came down the stairs. "Katie," Dad said, "you'll be amazed at how much the boys cleared out!"

"So, am I a good worker, or what?" Robert said.

"Hey, don't forget about me!" Jason said.

"You two make a good team!" Dad said. "Now let's get the stove moved and call it a day."

"Can I take Sara up to the tower?" I asked.

"Go ahead, but be careful. Here, take this flashlight," Dad said.

Now, with the boards off most of the windows, it was easier to see than it was yesterday. Sara followed me upstairs. "I'll keep an eye out for the you-know-what!" she said.

"Do you really think it would be right out in plain sight?" I asked.

"No. Not really," Sara said. "If it were in an easy place, somebody would have found it long ago."

"That's what I thought," I told her.

We reached the third floor. She followed me into the tower. "Well, what do you think?"

She giggled. "It would be a perfect place to leave a criminal. After you tied him up!"

"It's also a perfect place to be alone," I told her. "See how quiet it is?"

Sara listened. "It gives me the creeps!"

Personally, I was thinking how good it would be to sit up here and read. But Sara probably wouldn't understand.

"Look at how far down it is!" I rubbed the dirty window and looked down. My father, my brother, and Robert were standing next to the dumpster.

Suddenly, I grinned. "I have an idea!" I whispered in Sara's ear. She grinned, too. "Follow me!" I said.

We ran down to the second floor. I looked around for just the right thing. Aha! I pointed to a wooden box. She nodded. It would be perfect!

Sara helped me drag the box to the window.

51

"Quiet, now," I whispered.

She nodded and grinned.

Together we lifted the box to the window sill. And silently we pushed it out.

The crash into the dumpster was even louder than we'd hoped for!

The boys yelled. "Oh, no! That scared me to death!" Jason hollered.

While everybody looked up, Sara and I ducked down. We were laughing so hard we just had to sit down on the floor. It was the most fun I'd had all day!

Friends,
New and Old

"I can just walk back to town," Robert said. "It isn't far."

"Of course not. We'll take you home in Purple Jeep," Dad said.

"I wish I had my bike," he said. "I don't want you to feel you have to provide my transportation back and forth to the house."

Jason smiled. "Hey, you could use my bike! I'll be working here every day. I won't be using it."

I couldn't believe what I was hearing! Jason had earned the money for his 10-speed. And he wouldn't let me go anywhere near it. I looked at Dad, but he didn't say anything. He stuck the cleaning supplies inside the kitchen and locked the door.

"Are you sure, Jason?" Robert said. "I wouldn't want you to feel I was imposing or anything."

"We'll bring it tomorrow," my brother said. "OK, Dad?"

"That's fine," Dad said.

Actually, Robert was right. It wasn't very far into town. Although the boys sat together in the back seat, this time they didn't talk as much. I mean, I could even hear January snore.

"Just drop me off at the shopping center. I have to pick up something," Robert said.

"Would you like us to meet you here in the morning?" Dad asked. "About 8:30?"

Robert stood next to Purple Jeep and smiled. "Thank you, Sir. I'll be here."

Dad smiled. "Thanks for a good job. I think we're going to enjoy having you help us, Robert."

"My pleasure! Goodbye, Katie. See you tomorrow, Jason!" He stood there and waved as we drove off.

"What a neat guy!" Jason said. "I just wish he lived here. He'd make a great friend."

"Do you think the Lord sent him?" I asked.

Jason shrugged his shoulders. "How should I know?"

"It's just one more piece in the puzzle," Dad said. "God knows we need a home. I've never had a stronger sense of Him being in charge."

We were almost through town. As we headed north, suddenly I remembered Mom. "I wonder how Mom's doing."

"I've been thinking of her all day," Dad said. "It's hard to realize that any day now we'll be celebrating the arrival of a new baby!"

"Are you excited about the baby?" I asked.

"I certainly am!" Dad smiled.

"I hope it's a boy!" Jason said. I turned around to look at my brother. I haven't heard him say much about the baby.

"Lucky baby," I said. "He'll have four people to teach him things."

"And four people all set to love him." Dad smiled at me.

I thought about it. Dad was right. The most important thing would be to love him. Or her! I smiled, too.

Mom was waiting on the bench near the front door. When she saw us, she stood up. "Hi! I haven't gone to the hospital. I'm still here!"

Dad smiled. "So we see." He tried to hug her.

Mom laughed. She touched his face. "Just look at you! You look like you've been working in a coal mine!"

Dad laughed, too. "You're right, Elizabeth. I guess our next priority has to be water." But he didn't stop hugging her. "OK, Katie, you're first in the bathroom."

Fifteen minutes later we all were standing behind our chairs and holding hands. As usual, Dad started our song. "Praise God, from whom all blessings flow; Praise Him, all creatures here below ..."

"I'm starved," I said.

Mom smiled. "I thought you might be hungry enough for lasagna."

"Such a lot of work," Dad said. "Did you have time to do anything else?"

"Surprise!" Mom said. "I packed four more boxes. Penny Cochran came over for an hour after lunch and helped me."

"God sent us a helper, too!" Dad said.

"And a friend for Jason," I added.

Jason told Mom about Robert. "So I'm planning to take my bike along tomorrow. I won't be using it anyway. And Robert can ride it back and forth to town."

"Who is he staying with?" Mom asked.

"I don't know," Jason said. "He told me he has lots of relatives."

"Mom, my friend Sara came over. I took her up to the tower," I said.

"We'll have to watch those two girls," Dad laughed. "Somehow I have the feeling that what one of them doesn't think up, the other one will!" He smiled when he told Mom how we scared everybody.

"The boys scared us first," I said.

"Did you have the right supplies for the house?" Mom wondered.

"After lunch we picked up a few things at the hardware store," Dad explained. "As a matter of fact, that's how we found Robert."

"Mr. Snyder acts like he knows everything," Jason said. "He says everybody calls our place the Spook House. And he even tried to make us believe there's a treasure."

I held my breath.

Mom smiled. "Maybe we'll find it!"

"Oh, sure!" Jason laughed. "He must really think we're gullible!"

I couldn't look at my brother. I took a deep breath and reached for my glass of milk.

"I think I'd better have the water checked," Dad said. "I tried the pump, and it works. But it wouldn't hurt to have that checked, too. We'll need safe water for drinking."

"Is the stove hooked up?" Mom asked.

Dad shook his head. "Somebody capped the pipe. Actually, the gas is probably turned off anyway." He took out his notebook and wrote something down.

"Maybe I could come tomorrow and clean," Mom said.

"Let us get the worst of the dirt out first," Dad said. "I don't want you working that hard."

After supper, Jason and I always do the dishes. This week it's my turn to wash.

"Robert seems nice," I said.

Jason agreed. "He's shy—kind of hard to figure out."

"He didn't sound quiet in the car," I said.

"Oh, he talks a lot about the Broncos, and he knows a lot about houses," Jason said. "But when it comes to personal stuff, he clams up."

"Well, you hardly know him," I said. "Guess what? Today I found out that Sara Wilcox doesn't like to read."

"So?" He stopped drying and looked at me.

"So, nothing. It's just that I thought everybody likes to read."

"Lots of kids spend their time at home watching television," Jason said.

"Do you think when we move to town we'll get a TV?" I asked.

"We're probably too broke," Jason said. "And anyhow, we're always too busy to miss it."

After we finished in the kitchen, Jason went outside to tie his bike onto Purple Jeep. Mom and Dad were talking in the living room. Although it wasn't really time to go to bed, I climbed the ladder to the loft.

I went into my room and closed my door.

My dolls just sat there and looked at me. They didn't say a word.

"Hey," I told them. "Don't worry. You know I'll always love you."

But the dolls just sat there and watched me.

First I picked up Audrey, my Cabbage Patch doll, and gave her a hug. She's spunky. In fact, sometimes she even talks back. Now, she just smiled her weak little smile.

Next I hugged Gomer, my spineless stuffed lamb. Since he never really looks at you, it is hard to tell what he's thinking.

Last was Bronco Bob. I usually call him B. B. He always wears a big smile, no matter what.

I owed my friends an explanation. For days now, I've been rushing right past them.

"It's really special, don't you see?" I told the dolls. "Remember how I was praying for a real friend? Well, Sara Wilcox was praying for a friend, too. So the Lord stuck us together!"

Nobody said a word.

"Hey," I said, "you guys were my only friends for such a long time. I'll always love you!"

I can remember times when the four of us talked for hours. But now the dolls just looked at me.

Finally, I picked up Audrey again and hugged her. And then, while I stood there, I think I heard a tiny voice.

"We'll always love you, too," Audrey said.

I smiled and put her down.

We Start Searching for "It"

The next morning, when we reached Woodland Park, Robert was waiting at the shopping center—right where he said he'd be. "Good morning!" he said.

"I brought the bike," Jason said.

"So I see!" Robert climbed into the back seat with Jason. Even before Purple Jeep started to move, the two boys were talking.

"Jason's lucky to have Robert," I told Dad.

"Maybe Sara will come over," he said.

"If she does, can she help me work?"

"You mean like Robert?" Dad asked.

"Not exactly," I said. "I don't mean a regular job with money. But you could tell us what to do. And I'd have a partner to work with."

Dad smiled. "I think that could be worked out."

"Oh, thanks, Dad!" I felt wonderful.

When we first got to the house, I could hardly wait for Sara to arrive. The whole time I was sweeping the kitchen, I watched out the window. But there was no dog howling. No red hair.

"Sara isn't here?" Dad asked. He was cleaning out the bathroom, and he had to come out once in a while for air.

"Not yet," I sighed.

"You're doing a good job, Katie," he said. But even his praise didn't help me feel better.

Still, I kept sweeping. As my broom moved toward the corner of the kitchen, I coughed. I've never seen dirt so thick. And lots of it landed right back on me!

Upstairs I could hear the boys' footsteps and an occasional laugh.

"Good news!" Dad said, a little later. "We can use the bathroom! Just don't drink the water."

"Sara didn't show up," I told him.

My father nodded. "Maybe you could walk over to her house."

I looked at my dirty clothes. "I don't think so," I said.

"I'll be down soon," Dad said. "I'm going up to check on the boys."

I had just finished washing my hands when I

heard January's howl! I was so excited I just shook the water off and ran to the door!

AaaOoooooo!

Sara stood near the dumpster, her hands on her hips, and her red hair sticking up straight. "I knew this would happen!" she yelled. "I just knew it!"

AaaOoooooo! AaaOoooooo!

"Stop it, January!" I scolded. "It's just Sara!" The dog looked at her a long time. Then, with a weak whimper, he gave up.

"I think he's getting used to you," I said.

"Give me a break!" Sara said.

"I was waiting for you," I told her. "But then I thought you weren't coming."

"I was watching reruns," Sara said. "But to be honest, summer television isn't all that wonderful."

"Want to come in?" I asked. "Want to help me clean?"

"You mean *work?*" Sara asked. Slowly she put her hands back on her hips.

"What I'm doing here isn't exactly *work*," I said. "Besides, you're probably too skinny anyhow."

"Don't you dare call me skinny!"

"I'm sorry," I said. "What I meant was, you might not be strong enough. A Trash Buster has to be really strong."

"I'm as strong as you are, Katie Hooper!" Sara said. She started walking toward me.

"Also, you need experience," I told her.

"I can learn!" Sara said. "If you can do it, it can't be that hard!"

"Actually, being a Trash Buster is a huge honor!" I said.

Sara grinned at me. "Don't push your luck."

I grinned back. "OK. Come on in. I think maybe you'll do just fine!"

While we waited for Dad, I gave Sara a turn holding the dustpan. She started coughing. "Some honor!" she said.

I stopped sweeping. "I couldn't tell you this outside. Somebody might have heard me." I lowered my voice. "Being Trash Busters is part of my plan."

"Oh?"

"Yes," I told her. "See, if we weren't busy working, Dad might not want us inside the house. And then we'd never find it!"

She grinned. "You mean the you-know-what!" she said.

I nodded. "And with the kitchen almost finished, Dad will have to give us a better place to search!"

"Very clever," she said. "I didn't think you were that smart."

"I'm smarter than I look," I told her.

63

Dad came downstairs. "Oh," he said, "I see Sara's here!" He smiled at us.

"She wants to be a Trash Buster," I said. "But only if she can work with me!"

"I see," Dad said. "Is that right, Sara?"

She nodded.

"It just so happens that I need a couple of Trash Busters to sweep upstairs," Dad told us. "Jason and Robert have the junk cleaned out of two of the bedrooms."

Sara and I looked at each other. "Assignment accepted," I said.

Smiling, Dad handed Sara a broom. Then he turned to me. "Here," he said, "take these trash bags up with you. You can use them for any little stuff the boys missed."

Sara and I ran all the way upstairs. The back bedroom on the side above the dumpster was empty. As we passed in the hall, we could hear Jason and Robert talking in another room.

I looked around. Most of the furniture and other junk had already been thrown out the window. I opened up a plastic bag and carried it around, tossing in some newspapers, rags, a milk carton, and several tin cans.

Sara did nothing at all.

"You're supposed to help me," I told her.

"I'm busy," Sara whispered. "I'm looking for the you-know-what!" Suddenly, she pointed. In one corner of the room, the ceiling slanted. And underneath was a small door.

"In case somebody looks in, you can be sweeping," Sara told me. "I'll check out the door."

"Let's both sweep the room first," I said. "Then, if we're careful, we can both check out the door."

Immediately, sweeping became more exciting. When we were almost finished, Jason and Robert came in to throw a broken lamp out the window.

Robert looked at Sara. "You helping?" he asked.

"What does it look like?" Sara asked. Then she swept a cloud of dirt right at him.

"Ohhh, help, Jason!" Robert pretended to be afraid. Then he laughed and followed Jason out.

"That wasn't very nice," I told her.

"Sorry," Sara said. "But we can never do a proper search if those boys come poking around!"

"He wasn't poking," I said.

When we finished sweeping, we put our brooms in the corner and looked down the hall. The coast was clear.

We both knelt down in front of the little door. I was so excited I could hardly hold the flashlight. Sara turned the handle and slowly started to pull the door. It squeaked. Naturally! I felt like screaming.

Suddenly, Sara stopped and looked up at me. "If we find the secret treasure, we share it fifty-fifty!" she whispered. I nodded.

Behind the door, on the floor, was a carton not much bigger than a shoebox. Sara pulled it out slowly. "Where can we open it?" she asked. "If we do it here, somebody might see us."

I thought fast. "The bathroom," I said. "We'll open it in the bathroom."

The house was quiet. Since I'm more familiar with the layout, I was the scout. We really didn't need a scout. As Sara and I tiptoed through the hall, we didn't see a soul.

We closed the bathroom door. Sara set the box on the edge of the sink and lifted off the top.

The carton was filled with papers and note-books. We both looked underneath, but there was nothing else.

"Some treasure!" Sara said. "I'll be honest. I was hoping for gold!"

I was disappointed, too. But someone had to put this in perspective. "This can't be it!" I said. "But maybe this contains a clue! Are we going to give up just because we didn't find the treasure on the first try?"

"I guess not," Sara said.

We sneaked back to the bedroom. Then, right after we put the carton back, I froze. "Listen!" I said.

"I don't hear a thing," Sara said.

"That's just it," I told her. "I mean, is it deathly quiet, or what?"

"You win," she said. "It's deathly quiet."

Suddenly I remembered something. "Sara, I forgot to tell you something important!"

"You're just trying to psych me up so I won't quit working," she said.

"No, Sara, honest," I whispered. "I forgot all about it. I forgot to tell you that Jason found a secret passage!"

We Really Get Scared

When Sara's eyes get big, she looks like a clown. Maybe it's just her red hair. But it was hard to keep from laughing.

"Have you seen it—the secret passage?" Sara asked.

Giggling, I shook my head.

"What's so funny?" she wondered.

"Nothing, I guess."

Sara started to whisper. "We could spy on the boys."

I watched her eyes and tried not to laugh.

"Maybe they'll get careless and let their guard down and give us a clue. Right?"

I nodded.

"And then, when they go outside or to the

bathroom or something, we can search. OK?"

"Explain it again," I said. "Why do we have to spy on Jason and Robert?"

"I just told you! So we can try to find the secret passage."

"But I already know where it is!"

"You do?" She was surprised.

"It starts in the back of a closet," I told her. "I just don't know which one."

"Why didn't you say so?"

We looked at each other. The house was still quiet. "I don't hear anybody," I said. "Let's go!"

I went first. I tiptoed into the hall. Sara followed.

First, we looked inside the other empty bedroom. But it didn't have a regular closet. On one side we saw a large cabinet.

"It could be a closet in disguise," Sara said. But when we opened the doors, we saw that she was wrong.

The other front bedroom, the one with the awful green curtains, has a huge closet. As a matter of fact, it's bigger than lots of bedrooms. It even has two windows in it. But there's nothing that faintly resembles a secret passage.

"Maybe it's upstairs by the tower room," I suggested.

"Could be," Sara agreed. "But let's check that other room first."

The largest room on the second floor is at the rear of the house, to the right of the stairs. Because it has only two small windows in the far corners, it is also the darkest bedroom.

The room was still full of junk. I stumbled over a mangy old sleeping bag. And inside a glass jar was a half-burned candle! I pointed it out to Sara. She nodded.

We were making our way to the back wall and the only other door in the room. And, once again, I was starting to feel shaky.

"If you're scared, I'll open it," Sara said.

I nodded. "I'm not scared, but go on ahead," I said.

It was a closet, all right. Not a window in the whole area. I flashed the light around the walls. And there, in the back right corner, was a hole in the wall!

"Want to check it out?" Sara whispered.

I nodded. We were this far. It would be dumb not to keep going now.

"I'd better take the flashlight," Sara whispered. "Follow me."

The passageway was narrow, and it was low, and it was dark. We had to crawl on our hands and knees. "Don't go too fast," I said. "I can't see a thing."

Sara stopped. "Stick with me. The passageway turns."

"Did you just hear something?" I asked.

We froze. Sara turned off the flashlight, and we waited.

"I think I can see light ahead," she whispered.

We inched forward. Sara turned the corner. Then she started to scream! She tried to back up, but I was in the way. Naturally, I started screaming, too. The noise was deafening.

Finally, I was aware of another voice. "Katie, don't be afraid! Katie! Katie, it's just me! Katie, are you all right?"

"Sara, that's Jason's voice," I said. "It's just my brother!"

"Keep crawling, Katie," Jason said. "I'm in a kind of closet. Robert's with me. We won't hurt you!"

"It's OK," I told Sara. "Go on. Keep crawling. Then we can turn around and come back out!"

It wasn't easy. I mean Sara was just about as scared as you can get! But, finally, we crawled into the closet-like area at the far end of the secret passage.

"I was just showing this passageway to Robert," Jason explained. "We had no idea you would be coming."

"We're sorry!" Robert said. "Honest!"

And then we heard Dad's voice behind us. He sounded far away. "Katie, are you hurt? Are you all right?"

"She's OK, Dad," Jason called. "The girls got scared. But they aren't hurt or anything!"

It wasn't easy, but finally everybody ended up back in the bedroom. Dad's voice calmed me down, but Sara was crying.

"Katie," Dad said, in a quiet voice, "take hold of Sara's hand." I reached over and obeyed. "Now, let's all go downstairs."

We didn't stop walking until we were standing on the back porch.

"We're so sorry!" Dad told Sara. "Being afraid is an awful feeling, isn't it!"

Sara nodded. She held on tightly to my hand. "I hate this Spook House," she said. "And I hope I never have another adventure in my entire life!"

"You can go home if you want to, Sara," Dad told her. "Want Katie to go with you?"

Sara's lip trembled. "I'm afraid to go home. There's nobody there."

"We're going to have a picnic lunch," Dad told her. "We'd like to have you stay and eat with us."

"Do you like Hershey bars?" I asked. "Mom put in Hershey bars for dessert."

Sara nodded. "They're my favorite."

After lunch, Dad smiled at me. "You know, I've been thinking. I could use some help out here in the yard! Any chance the Trash Busters might work out here this afternoon?"

I looked at Sara.

"I feel lots better," she said.

So Sara and I spent most of the afternoon running around in the weeds picking up trash in the yard.

Later, as Sara lugged a rusty bicycle wheel toward the dumpster, she stopped. "It probably wasn't in there anyhow," she said.

"What wasn't in there?" I asked.

Sara grinned. "You know," she said, "the treasure. If it had been in the secret passageway, the boys would have found it anyway!"

Later, when Sara went home, I asked Dad if I could spend some time up in the little tower before we left.

"Sure," he smiled. "You've been working hard all day. I think some time to yourself would be a good thing."

On the way up, I passed Jason and Robert. Since lunch, they had been working on the first floor. They had cleared out most of the room in front of the kitchen. Now they couldn't just drop things out the window. They had to carry the trash onto the porch and throw it into the dumpster.

On the second floor, I stopped off in the rear bedroom. This time, as I opened the little door, I wasn't afraid. Glancing around to make sure nobody was watching, I reached inside and pulled out the carton. Then I carried it with me up to the tower.

When I entered the tower, I realized I was smiling. It was funny. I had exactly the same feeling as when I go back to my own room in our cabin. I felt like I had come home.

Although the turret hasn't been cleaned out, it isn't nearly as full of junk as the rooms on the lower two floors. I sat on the floor in the corner and pulled a letter out of the box.

That's when I discovered how hard it is to read the handwriting! Believe me, this is the most *cursive* writing I've ever seen in my life. I'll bet even my teacher would have trouble reading this!

The front of the carton contained letters and postcards. Each envelope was addressed to Dr. and Mrs. Frank Willard. That figured. No wonder some people called our house the old *Willard* place!

I looked at another letter. Same thing. *Dr. and Mrs. Frank Willard.* And suddenly it sank in. Our house had been owned by a doctor! And I realized he must have been a rich doctor to build such a big house!

I didn't even try to read the letters. I stacked them back in the front of the box. Unfortunately, the notebooks were also difficult to read. I flipped through pages of dates and lists. Most of the words were long. And the handwriting was full of curlicues.

Then, suddenly, I spotted a short word! *Gold!* It couldn't have been plainer! I couldn't read the rest of that line. But there it was again, two lines down. It said *Gold!*

That's when I heard Dad calling. I put everything back and carried the box down to its hiding place in the second floor closet. Then I ran all the way downstairs.

I had discovered two things. The owner of our house had been a doctor. And Dr. Willard had had something to do with gold!

I had been right. The box did contain clues. And if Sara and I weren't too scared, the possibility of treasure no longer seemed like just a dream!

Sara Finds Courage

Robert was unlocking Jason's bike from the tree when the rest of us started out to Purple Jeep. "Jason, it was great of you to bring your bike for me to use!" Robert said. "Don't worry. I'll take good care of it!"

"Please be careful on the highway," Dad told him.

Robert smiled. "I'll be careful."

Just before Dad pulled away, Jason called, "See you tomorrow."

Robert waved.

"How come you showed Robert the secret passage?" I asked my brother.

"Why not?" Jason replied. "He's my friend. You were showing Sara!"

"She was really scared," I said.

"Tell me about it!" Jason said. "I've never heard such a scream! Did you stop to think how Robert and I felt!"

I shook my head and looked at my brother. "You were scared?" I asked.

"Well," Jason said, "not exactly scared, but we sure were surprised!"

"You were scared!" I said.

Jason looked at me and grinned.

* * * * * * * *

At supper, Dad told Mom about our progress at the house. "Maybe having Robert's help has made the difference. But we're much farther along than I expected to be!"

"I can't wait any longer!" Mom said. "Tomorrow I'm going with you. I have to see for myself."

* * * * * * * *

Today was our basic Colorado morning. The air was crisp, and the sun felt warm on my cheeks. I think even January enjoyed the drive down the mountain. At least he stayed awake.

"I have such a good feeling about our move," Mom said. "I just know we're going to be happy in our new home!"

Dad parked in front of the house and almost bounded out of Purple Jeep. For such a big man, he really can move! He hurried around to help Mom. Smiling, he said, "I'm as excited as you are, Elizabeth!"

"Guess what?" Jason said. "Robert's here already! I can see my bike."

When we reached the back porch, Robert was sitting on the step eating a granola bar.

"Hi, Robert," Jason said. "I want you to meet my mom."

Immediately, Robert rose to his feet. I thought he seemed embarrassed. At first, he didn't say anything.

Mom smiled at him. "Hi, Robert," she said. "I've been hearing about what good help you are."

"Yes, Ma'am," he said. "The old house is beginning to look a lot different!"

"You're here awfully early," Mom said. "I hope your family understands."

Robert smiled. "We still have a lot of work to do before you can move in," he said.

"Today I want you boys to try to repair the broken windows," Dad said. "I'll get you started as soon as I show off our progress to the lady of the house."

When Mom and Dad went inside, Robert sat down again. Jason sat down next to him.

"Steve, it's a miracle!" Mom entered the kitchen and squealed with delight. I grinned. I hurried in so I could hear her reactions.

Soon my parents were standing in the room directly in front of the kitchen.

"I agree, Steve," Mom was saying. "This will make a wonderful dining room. I can't believe it's all cleared out already!"

"Remember, I don't want you working too hard today, Elizabeth," Dad said.

"Don't worry about me!" Mom assured him. "I'll take plenty of breaks when I get tired. There aren't that many kitchen cabinets to clean out."

"Before we go upstairs, I'd like your opinion on these other two rooms," Dad said. "Which shall we clean out first?"

In addition to the kitchen and dining room, there are two other rooms on the first floor. One is in front of the stairway, and the bigger one is in back. Actually, they are right underneath two of the bedrooms.

Mom walked into the hall and looked into each room. "This can be the parlor," she said. "And the one in back can be our family room. Why don't you do that room first."

"Excellent," Dad said. Then he realized I was there. "Well, Katie," he said, "is your fellow Trash Buster coming back to help?"

"I hope Sara can forget about her scare," I said.

"I hope so, too," Dad agreed. "Do you want to keep working in the yard? That way, you can watch for her."

"That's a good idea," I said. When my parents went upstairs to see the bedrooms, I went back outside. Jason and Robert had disappeared.

"Good dog," I said to January. He was, as usual, at his post next to the dumpster. I tossed in a beer can.

Then I ran into the front yard and tried to move a big tire. Because it was too heavy for me to drag back to the dumpster, I started making a pile of junk. While I waited for Sara, I had to do something.

Luckily, I didn't have to wait long. Sara saw me as soon as I saw her. We ran toward each other.

My friend looked exactly the same as she did yesterday. She wore the same pink jogging shoes. She even had on the same *Cool Colorado* tee shirt. And her red hair still stuck up straight. I honestly don't think she could comb her hair if she tried!

We stood grinning at each other. "I wasn't sure you'd come," I said.

"I saw you working outside," she said. "Even if I help you, cleaning up this yard will take forever!"

"No television this morning!"

"Nope." She smiled. "I'll have to admit it. Real life at the Hoopers' is more exciting!"

"My mom's here today," I said. "I'd like you to meet each other!"

"Where is she?"

"Inside," I said. "She's going to clean the kitchen cabinets."

"I'm not so sure I want to go in that house again," Sara admitted.

"Do you still feel that way?" I asked.

"I think so."

"Oh," I said. I took a few steps, picked up a board with nails in it, and tossed it on the junk pile.

"Feel like racing?" Sara asked. "I'll beat you to the tree!" She got such a good start I couldn't catch her.

"Wait up," I yelled. When I reached her, we both were out of breath. "Sara, I have something neat to tell you."

"What?" she asked.

"I found some clues," I said. "Maybe there really is a secret treasure!"

"Shhhhh!" Sara glanced around to see if anybody was nearby. Personally, I thought it was kind of dumb. There was nobody around for miles. Everyone else was inside the house. But Sara lowered her voice. "OK," she whispered, "what did you find?"

"After you left, I took that carton out of the closet," I said.

"I hope nobody saw you!"

"Nobody did," I said. "I went up to the turret."

"Where?"

"The little tower room," I said. "Remember? The other place that gives you the creeps!"

"Don't make fun of me," Sara said. "Can I help it if I'm nervous?"

"Guess what? I discovered that our house used to belong to a rich doctor," I said. "His records tell about *gold!*"

"No kidding!" Sara forgot to whisper. "It's funny, but all along, I was kind of hoping for gold!"

"It's too bad," I said. "Because, of course, you'll probably never be in on finding it. Since you're probably too scared to keep looking!"

"Well, I'll admit I was pretty frightened yesterday!" Sara said.

"You acted like you were scared to death!"

"You're right," she said. "I was never that scared before in my entire life. Could you tell?"

"I could tell," I said. "And I felt awful about it. I can certainly understand why you might never want to go back inside that house!"

"On the other hand, I don't want to keep on being afraid forever," Sara said. "When you stop and think about it, there wasn't any real danger."

"You're right," I said.

"Actually, it was just Jason and Robert," she continued.

I nodded.

"And the truth is, I'm really not afraid of Jason and Robert!"

I grinned at Sara. She grinned back.

"Then come on!" I said. "What are we waiting for?"

We Find Mom's Treasure

We went in the back door and found my mother in the kitchen. "Hi, Mom. This is Sara."

My mother put her sponge into the dirty water and dried her hands. "Hi, Sara," she said. "It's good to meet you. Katie's been telling me about you."

"She didn't tell me about *you*," Sara said. "You're going to have a baby!"

Mom smiled. "Yes, I am! We're all excited about it!"

Sara turned to me. "How come you didn't tell me?" she asked.

"There's lots of things I haven't told you," I said. "It just never came up. You haven't told me about your mother either!"

"There's nothing much to tell about my mother. She certainly isn't going to have a baby!" Sara said.

"I have an idea, Sara," Mom said. "When we move into this house, you can come over here and share our baby."

Sara's eyes got big. "Really?" she said.

Mom smiled. "Really!"

"In case you want to know, I never really planned to come into this house again!" Sara said. Sometimes she is very dramatic. Maybe it's because she watches so much television.

"I forgot to tell you about it, Mom," I said. "Yesterday Sara got scared."

"You got scared, too!" Sara said.

"Not as scared as you did!"

"Hey," Mom laughed. "It doesn't really matter. Are you both full of courage now?"

"We are," I told her. "Why?"

"When I finish washing out this cabinet, I'd like to organize a treasure hunt!" Mom said.

I couldn't believe it!

"No fair, Katie!" Sara said. "I can't believe you told her!"

"I didn't tell her," I said.

"Oh, my," Mom said. "Let me explain what I meant, Sara. You see, the Hoopers often have treasure hunts."

"It's true," I told Sara. "It's a kind of game my

family plays. The last time we did it, Dad drew pictures for clues. And the treasure turned out to be our supper!"

Sara just looked at me.

"It was more fun than it sounds," I said.

Mom laughed. "Katie's right, Sara. You really had to be there!"

"So when does the game start?" Sara asked. "And who's making up the clues this time?"

"Oh, my," Mom said. Then her voice got very quiet. She can be every bit as dramatic as Sara. "When I looked at the house this morning, I saw something I hadn't noticed before!"

"The dumpster?" I guessed.

"Well, that too," Mom said. "But for the first time, I noticed a chimney."

"Oh," I said. "A chimney."

Mom continued. "And I thought to myself, 'I wonder why there's a chimney going up the side of that porch?'" Mom smiled. "Now, girls, when you think of a chimney, what does that remind you of?"

"Santa Claus?" Sara said. "Do you Hoopers believe in Santa Claus?"

"Of course not," I said. "She's probably thinking about a fireplace. Right?"

"That's exactly what I'm thinking," Mom said. "Let's check out the dining room! Do you see anything that looks like a fireplace?"

We both ran and looked.

"Mom!" I got excited. "There are bricks on the floor over here!"

"And look! The wall sticks out funny!" Sara said.

"You two are wonderful detectives!" Mom said. She had followed us into the dining room. "It looks like a big piece of plasterboard has been nailed up across that wall."

"Maybe Dad can pull it off," I said.

"Your father's taken the boys to town to get glass for the windows," Mom said. "Maybe we can surprise them!"

"Yes, let's surprise them!" I said.

"How?" Sara asked.

"Well," Mom said, "we'll have to punch a hole in the wall and see what's behind there. I think you girls can do the work. Why don't you see if you can find a hammer."

Sara and I raced around. We finally found Dad's tools and returned with two hammers. I got the bigger one.

"OK," Mom said. "Stand over there and try to knock a hole right above those bricks."

I swung my hammer against the wall. It made a noise, but nothing else happened. "Your turn," I told Sara.

"I'll never make a hole with this puny hammer," she said. She turned to Mom. "Are you sure it's all right to be doing this?"

"I'm sure," Mom said. "I think it's hollow. Keep pounding on the same place!"

I did. Soon dust was flying all over. And the wall was beginning to crack. And, finally, my hammer went right through!

"OK, Sara, pound right next to the hole. Make the hole bigger!" Mom said.

In no time at all, we had a hole in the wall the size of a baseball.

"It better be a fireplace," Sara said. "What if it isn't?"

"That's a good point," Mom said. "I think you'd better check it out."

But when I tried to look inside, I couldn't see a thing. "We'd better get the flashlight," I said.

"Good thinking," Mom replied. "Isn't this fun!"

Sara found the flashlight, and we ran back to the dining room. "I can't tell what's behind there," she said. "I think it's full of junk."

"Let me look," Mom said. She had a hard time bending down. "Girls, it's a fireplace, all right! Keep pounding!"

It was the most fun I've had in my whole life! We laughed, and we sang, and we pounded. And Mom laughed and sang right along with us!

"You're a neat mother!" Sara said. "If you want to know, I never saw a mother like you before!"

Mom just laughed.

"Well, what have we here?" Dad's voice surprised us, and we stopped pounding.

"It's a fireplace!" Mom said. "The girls found a fireplace!"

"What a surprise!" Dad said.

"What a mess!" Robert laughed.

"Let me help you!" Jason said as he reached for my hammer.

"No!" I yelled. "This is our project! This is our treasure hunt. Mom said!"

"She's right, boys," Dad told them. "Your job is to repair windows. You can watch the girls a few minutes, but then we have to get started."

"Thank you, Steve," Mom said. "When we need some help, we'll ask."

"Dad, maybe you could get the high part," I said. "We're too short!"

Dad looked around and laughed. "Here I thought you girls were Trash Busters! Look at this room! From now on, I'll have to call you Trash Makers!"

"We'll clean it up, Mr. Hooper," Sara said.

So Sara and I kept pounding. Actually, later on, Dad did help some. But not the boys. They worked on the front porch glazing windows.

After a long time, Sara and I got so hot and tired that Mom invited us to stop for a cold drink. We went out on the back steps so we could sit down.

While we were taking our break, we could hear my parents talking in the kitchen.

"Is something wrong, Steve?" Mom asked.

"I'm not sure," Dad said. "Robert's acting strange today. First, he was very reluctant to go into town with us. And then he wouldn't come into the hardware store."

"Did you ask him about it?" Mom asked.

"He says he just wants to keep working on the house. He's worried that we won't get moved in before the baby comes," Dad said.

Sara was listening, too. "What if you don't get moved in?" she asked me. "Do you ever think about that?"

I shook my head. "My parents said it's the Lord's problem. I know everything will work out OK."

"I'm glad you didn't tell your mother about the other treasure," Sara whispered.

"It's our secret, yours and mine," I said. "I never even told Jason!"

"Good," Sara said. "We won't tell anybody! And especially we won't tell Robert!"

All in a Day's Work

By the end of the day, Sara and I were sweeping up the plaster dust mess. And we had discovered a wonderful fireplace in our dining room!

The fireplace we found today is nothing like the one in our cabin. That one is built into a stone wall, with a big beam across for a mantel. This fireplace is built right into the plastered wall. Around the edge and across the top is an old wooden framework painted blue. Mom said the shelf at the top is also called a mantel.

Actually, Mom was thrilled! "The Lord is so good!" she kept saying. "Somehow I could face leaving our lovely cabin. But it was hard for me to imagine living without a fireplace. And now the Lord has given me the desire of my heart!"

For Sara, today's hard work was more like wild and glorious fun. But I couldn't help thinking that she envied me. And not just about the baby either! All day long Sara kept saying, "I can't believe your mother!" And sometimes she would say things like, "Katie, do you know how lucky you are to have a mother like that!"

By afternoon, I realized how right Sara was. What a difference! Just having Mom here today turned the old house into a real home! I started to picture our family life here. I imagined cookie smells in the kitchen. I could picture all of the Hoopers standing behind our chairs in the dining room singing "Praise God, from whom all blessings flow!" And then I imagined my friend Sara waiting for me out on the back steps!

In Dad's case, today was a day of relief. "Elizabeth, we're going to make it!" he kept saying. "At first, I wasn't sure. The house seemed like too big a project to handle! But now, I can look around and see all that we've done already. And what's left to do seems possible! I just know we're going to make it!"

For Jason, this was a day of learning and accomplishment. "I did this window myself!" he said. "Just think! When I woke up this morning, I didn't know a thing about repairing a broken window. And now, thanks to Robert, I'm practically an expert glazer! Maybe I'll even be able to get a job after school!"

And, as the day progressed, I noticed that Robert seemed happier and more relaxed. "I'm not really such a wonderful teacher," he told Jason at lunchtime. "You learn fast!"

"You've put in glass before!" Mom said. "Where did you learn so much about old houses?"

Robert smiled. "From my father," he said. "He's a contractor. He does a lot of work for people who are fixing up older homes. Most of them can't afford new houses."

"Older places have more charm anyway," Mom said. "They're full of surprises!"

"Like fireplaces!" I said.

"Exactly!" Mom grinned.

By late afternoon, when Dad came in to tell us it was time to think about going home, Sara was still helping me. But frankly, I think she mostly wanted to be near my mother!

"Are you coming back tomorrow?" Sara asked.

"Of course," I said.

"Will your mother be coming?" she asked.

"I don't know," I said.

"She might have the baby tonight!" Sara said.

"I guess she could."

"I'm going to ask her," Sara said.

"Ask her what?" I wondered.

"If she's going to have the baby tonight!"

At first, Mom laughed. But then she realized that Sara was serious. "You don't know very much about babies, do you?" she said gently.

"I know enough," Sara said. But then she shook her head. "Well, not very much," she admitted.

"A baby is a special gift from God," Mom told her. "Usually people don't know a baby's birthday ahead of time."

"Does God know?" Sara asked.

"I'm sure He does," Mom said. "But it's like a lot of other things. God doesn't always tell us everything He knows!"

"I get it," Sara said. "He likes to surprise us!"

Mom smiled. "I think you're right," she said.

"I hope you'll be here again tomorrow," Sara said. "But if you aren't, I'll know why!"

Mom laughed. "Wait a minute, Sara. I could just be up at the cabin packing for our move!"

"Oh," Sara said.

Outside, Robert had unlocked Jason's bike. "I'm going to start for town," he said. "I'll see you tomorrow."

"Just a minute, Robert," Mom said. "I've been wanting to ask you something."

Robert looked down at the bike.

"Is your whole family staying in Woodland Park? We'd like to meet them sometime."

"It's just my father and me," Robert said. "I

mean, that's all that's in my family. And Dad's still in Denver."

"So who are you staying with?" Mom asked.

"Friends," Robert said.

"We probably should have their address and phone number," Mom said. "We might need to contact you."

"Like if you have the baby or something?" Robert asked.

Mom laughed. "Sometimes I think you and Sara are more anxious about our baby than we are!"

"I'm not so sure, Elizabeth!" Dad's eyes twinkled.

We watched Robert ride off.

Dad turned to Jason. "Does he talk about his father much?"

Jason shook his head. "Hardly at all."

"That boy is hiding something," Mom said. "There's something he isn't telling us."

"Like a secret?" I asked.

Sara poked me. "Katie, don't you dare tell!"

"I won't!" I said.

"Katie has a secret!" Jason chanted. "Katie has a secret!"

"I do not!" I said.

"Do, too!" my brother teased. "Katie can't keep a secret. She never could!"

"I can, too!" I said.

"Remember when you told Dad what you made him for Christmas!" Jason said.

"That's enough, Jason!" Dad warned. "Katie didn't tell me. I just happened to guess."

"Oh, sure!" Jason laughed. "You just happened to guess she made a leather bookmark!"

"That will do," Mom said. "If we don't get started, we might run into traffic."

"OK, gang. Load the stuff into Purple Jeep," Dad said. "I'll walk through and check the house before I lock up."

Sara waited around until we were ready to drive off. "See you tomorrow!" She stood next to the road and waved until we couldn't see her anymore.

"Let's watch for Robert!" Jason said. "When we pass him, we can honk and wave." But we never did see him. He must have had too good a start.

As we drove north out of Woodland Park, Mom was still enthusiastic. "The Lord is so good! Just think, Steve, a fireplace!"

It had been a wonderful day. Everybody in the family was smiling. That is, everybody except January. As usual, he was asleep.

Sara Gets Scared Again

This morning, Mom changed her mind about coming with us and stayed at the cabin. As it turned out, it probably was just as well!

It was another beautiful day, and Dad was in a good mood—until we got nearly to Woodland Park. Then, while he was explaining about having the electricity at the house hooked up, we had trouble with the car.

"What's wrong?" Jason asked. Purple Jeep coughed twice and then was silent. Dad steered as we coasted to a stop on the side of the road.

"I think we're out of gas," Dad said.

I remembered last night. Mom had wanted him to stop for gas on the way home.

At first, Dad didn't say anything. He turned

the key and tried to start the motor, but nothing happened. "I'll have to hike into town," he said. "You two can wait here."

"I'll go with you, Dad," Jason offered.

"No, thanks. We can't leave Katie here alone."

"I'll come, too," I said.

"Then we'd have to take January," Dad said. "It would be a regular caravan! No, I'll go by myself. I'll come back as soon as I can." After pulling the brake, he looked around for approaching cars and got out.

Jason and I watched our father lope down the road. He wasn't smiling.

"He should have listened to Mom," Jason said.

"That won't help now," I said. "Besides, you know how he hates being wrong!"

"You going to tell Mom?" he asked.

I shook my head. "Are you?"

January opened one eye, looked at me, and then went back to sleep.

"I've been thinking," Jason said. "I wonder if the house has more secret passages?"

I was surprised. "Really! Do you think there might be others?"

"I don't know," he said. "Doesn't it seem strange that in a few days we've already found a passageway and a fireplace?"

I nodded. "Where else could we look?"

"I don't know. I guess the cellar is one possibility. But I hate even the thought of going down there!" Jason said.

"Really! Me, too!"

"Still, I can't help but think that the first passage ought to lead *somewhere!*"

"The fireplace and the passageway can't be connected," I said. "They are on opposite sides of the house."

"I know," Jason said. "I already thought of that."

"You did?"

"Of course. I've been doing a lot of thinking about the house. Did you think you and Sara are the only ones looking for secrets?" he asked.

"I guess not," I said slowly. "How did you know about it?"

"How did I know about what?"

I stopped. "You're just trying to trap me! You're trying to find out our secret!"

Jason laughed. "I almost did it, didn't I?"

"You're impossible!" I laughed, too.

A pickup truck stopped across the road, and Dad got out. He was carrying a red gasoline can. "Thanks a lot!" he said. He waved as the truck drove on.

By the time we got to the house, we were almost an hour late. "I hope Robert waited for us," Jason said. "He must have thought we weren't coming."

"The bike's there," Dad said.

As we reached the back porch, we saw Robert picking up junk in the back yard. He ran over to us before Dad got the kitchen door unlocked. "You're later than usual!" he said. "I thought maybe you took Mrs. Hooper to the hospital!"

"No, she's working back at the cabin," Jason explained.

"Sorry we're late," Dad said. "We had some minor car trouble."

I glanced at Jason. But neither of us said a word.

"Today, I'd like you boys to clear out the trash from the back room," Dad said. "Mrs. Hooper wants to use it as our living room." All of us followed him through the hall and into the big room in the rear of the house.

"We still have a few more windows to do," Jason remembered.

"We can finish putting them in later," Dad said.

"What do you want Sara and me to do?" I asked.

"You girls can finish sweeping upstairs," Dad said. "The trash is cleared out of the big bedroom."

Jason and Robert started working right away. I headed out to the rear porch to wait for Sara. But she didn't show up. I hung around for a while waiting. But finally I had to go upstairs by myself.

It was the first time I had been in the back bedroom since Sara and I crawled into the secret passageway. In my mind, I could still remember her blood-curdling scream!

But now everything was quiet. I started sweeping in the far corner of the room, next to the window. When I got to the closet door, I bravely decided to pull it open.

I was startled to hear voices. Although I tried to listen, I couldn't make out who was talking or what the voices were saying.

That's when I realized that the big back room on the first floor was right underneath me. Of course! The biggest bedroom was directly above the big living room. And then I knew that the voices I heard had to belong to Jason and Robert! Naturally!

I had just picked up my broom again when I heard a faint howling sound. *AaaOoooooo!* I couldn't believe it! I honestly thought that January had stopped howling at Sara! I rushed downstairs.

AaaOoooooo!

On the way out, I passed Dad in the kitchen. "I guess Sara's here," he smiled.

Sure enough! It was Sara, all right. But she was standing halfway across the yard. "Come on over!" I called. "I'll quiet January down!"

"I'm not coming," Sara called.

"Why not?" I yelled.

AaaOoooooo! AaaOoooooo!

"Be quiet," I told January. "Can't you see it's just my friend Sara!"

AaaOooooo!

I looked over at Sara. She was not coming toward the house. In fact, if anything, she was moving backwards!

I tried to remember what trick I had used before to quiet January down. Firmness! I think I had been firm. But when I tried firmness, nothing happened. The stupid dog kept howling.

Finally, my father appeared. "What's going on out here?"

"I'm not sure," I said. "I can't make January stop howling. And Sara's way over there!"

AaaOoooooo!

"Enough, January!" Dad hollered. That did the trick. The dog stopped howling and started whining.

"OK, Sara!" I called. "Come on! The coast is clear!"

"I'm not coming!" Sara hollered. "You come here!"

Honestly! But I had no choice. While the dog whined and Dad went back into the house, I started down the back porch steps.

Sara didn't move an inch closer while I ran toward her. "Sara, what's going on?"

"I've had it!" she said. "I'm positively never going into that house again! And what's more, Katie Hooper, I don't even care if you do find the treasure all by yourself!"

"Sara," I asked, "what's wrong?"

"It isn't worth it," she said.

"What isn't worth it? You aren't afraid of January, are you?"

Sara shook her head. "No, it isn't January."

"But you are afraid?"

She nodded.

"But it was only Jason and Robert in the passageway," I reminded her. "And you know you aren't afraid of them."

"I know," Sara said. "Katie, this was worse. A million times worse!"

"Tell me," I said. "Did something happen before we got here this morning?"

"Not this morning," Sara gasped. Her eyes got big. "It was last night. That's when I saw it."

"Saw what?"

Sara took a deep breath. "I was on my way home last night. And I was walking past your house."

"Yes? What happened, Sara?"

"It was almost dark. I was just thinking how glad I was that you're going to live here. That's

105

when I looked up at your tower." Sara paused. "And that's when I saw it!"

"Saw what?" I asked again. I was beginning to get impatient!

"The ghost!" Sara whispered. "Right in your tower window. I saw a ghost!"

"No, Sara," I said. "It couldn't have been a ghost."

"Oh, yes it was!" Sara insisted. "So now I know all those stories about Spook House are true. Katie, your house is haunted!"

What Did Sara See?

Sara stuck to her story. I couldn't talk her out of it. And no amount of persuasion would get her to come back into Home Sweet Home.

When I walked back to the house alone, Dad was helping the boys load an old mattress into the dumpster. "Where's Sara?" he asked.

"She won't come," I said. "She's afraid to come back into the house."

"I bet she's just disappointed that Mom isn't here today," Jason said. "She really likes Mom."

"That's not it," I said. "She saw something here last night that scared her."

"Oh?" Dad said. "What did Sara see?"

I felt sort of silly even saying it. "She thinks she saw a ghost," I told them.

Well, you should have heard those boys laugh! In fact, suddenly, I kind of felt like giggling myself.

"She's probably tired of working," Jason said. "My guess is that she's taking a day off to play!"

"What an imagination!" Robert said. "She's quite an actress, isn't she!"

"Maybe it comes from watching a lot of television," I said.

Well, whatever the reason for Sara's decision, I really missed her. Somehow nothing I did alone was half the fun. After lunch, I even worked in the yard, in the hope that she'd see me and come over.

But Sara was gone all right. And the more I thought about it, the more I decided the boys were wrong. Sara really had been frightened!

I tried to get my spirits up by thinking about the secret treasure. But, without Sara, even that seemed kind of boring. Besides, I couldn't even read the clues. So the doctor had a thing for gold! So what!

By the end of the day, I was such a gloomy gus that Dad suggested I might want to spend some time up in the turret.

I agreed. "Call me when you're ready to go home," I said.

Since I didn't have a book to read, I decided I might as well stop on the second floor to pick up the carton of clues. Maybe today I'd have better luck reading them! Actually, if I found out some more about the gold, maybe Sara would even change her mind!

I figured I didn't have to be real careful. Jason and Robert had been working on the first floor all day long, so I didn't think anyone would see me. I walked right into the back bedroom, stooped down to open the little door, and reached in for the box.

It wasn't there! I knelt down and waved my arm back and forth. No carton. It couldn't just disappear!

Frankly, I was starting to get a little scared myself. I quickly closed the little door and ran downstairs.

"Back so soon?" Dad asked. "We aren't ready to leave yet. I'll call you, Katie."

"Can I borrow your flashlight?" I asked.

This time the little door squeaked, and my courage nearly failed me. But I held my breath and shone the light inside.

The carton was there after all. But someone had pushed it way over to the left side!

And something navy blue was rolled up and stuck in on the right. It looked exactly like a sleeping bag.

I closed the little door and nearly banged my head on the sloping ceiling. This time I walked slowly down the stairs.

I wondered what I should do now. I'm not exactly an expert on ghosts. But personally, I doubt very much that a ghost would need a sleeping bag!

On the other hand, if it wasn't a ghost Sara saw in the turret, who was it?

When I got downstairs, Dad was nearly ready to leave. Back at the cabin, Mom was fixing a picnic, and he was anxious to get started. Robert had already gone.

"Feeling better, Katie?" Dad asked, as we started for home.

"Sort of," I said.

"Sara will probably come back tomorrow," Dad said.

"Oh, look, there's Robert! Dad, can you slow down?" Jason yelled.

Robert was pedaling along the right side of the road. Since this is all uphill, he wasn't going very fast. Dad pulled Purple Jeep off the road right ahead of him.

"Hi, Robert!" Jason said. You'd never have guessed that the two had worked side by side all day long!

"Well, if it isn't the Hoopers!" Robert was smiling.

"We're having a picnic tonight, Robert," Dad said. "I didn't think of it before, but why don't you join us? I'm sure my wife has plenty of food for everyone."

Robert's smile faded. "Thank you," he said. "I wish I could, but I have other plans tonight."

"Maybe another time," Dad said.

With lots of smiling and waving, we headed north. I turned and looked back. Robert had gotten off Jason's bike and was now walking up the steep grade.

"Cheer up, Katie," Jason said. "Your friend Sara will be back tomorrow!"

I smiled. But I wasn't so sure.

* * * * * * * *

When we reached the cabin, Mom had everything packed in our picnic basket. "If you're not too tired, I thought we'd eat by the stream," she said.

"Maybe I could just throw a line in the water," Dad said.

"Why not?" Mom smiled.

It was a great supper. Mom had even fried chicken. "I wanted this picnic to be special! Once the baby arrives, we can always eat sandwiches!" she laughed. Fried chicken is one of our Hooper family traditions. When Mom was a girl in Illinois, *her* mother used to fry chicken for picnics.

After we ate, while Dad and Jason fished, I helped Mom pick up. "You're awfully quiet, Katie," she said. "Is something wrong?"

She can always guess. "Not exactly. I've been thinking about Sara," I said.

"She'll probably be back tomorrow," Mom said.

I sighed. "Nobody understands, Mom. I'm the only one who talked to Sara, and I saw how scared she was! Honestly, Mom, she saw something!"

"This happened last night?"

"That's right," I said. "She said it was just getting dark. And she looked up at our turret window and saw a ghost."

"Sara is pretty dramatic," Mom said.

"I know," I admitted. "But that doesn't prove she didn't see anything."

"True," Mom agreed.

"People have been telling scary stories about our house," I said. "Did you know that?"

"Yes," Mom said. "That happens almost every time a house is empty for a long time."

"It's no use," I said. "Nobody will believe me."

"There's something else, isn't there?" Mom asked. "Something you haven't told me?"

I nodded. I hadn't mentioned the clues or the closet to anybody. "But, Mom, I can't tell. Because if I do, I'll be giving away a secret."

"I see," Mom said. She closed the picnic basket.

"Katie, you really think Sara saw something in our house last night, don't you?"

"I do," I said. "But I can't prove it or anything."

"I have an idea," Mom said. "See what you think of this. Suppose we all drive down there tonight and check the place out?"

"Really! You'd do that?" I asked.

"Certainly," Mom said. "It's a beautiful night for a drive. And you know me. I'm always ready for an adventure!"

"What about Dad and Jason?" I asked.

"Leave that to me," Mom grinned. "They can stay at the cabin and miss the adventure if they want to. But I have a feeling they'll come along!"

"Sara's right," I said. "You really are a special mother!"

Mom hugged me. "Is this the first time you noticed?" she teased.

"Of course not," I said. And I hugged her back.

We Catch Our Ghost

Mom guessed right. Dad and Jason didn't want to miss out on anything. And, as usual, everybody picked up Mom's enthusiasm.

"We might as well catch a ghost," Dad laughed. "The fish sure aren't biting!"

We stopped briefly at the cabin to drop off January and get extra flashlights. "I think each of us should have one," Mom said. "It's going to be dark!"

Even Jason was really into the adventure. "I've always thought it would be exciting to be a detective," he said. "Besides, it will be cool to see the old house at night!"

Although everybody was plenty excited, nobody was really scared. Except me.

114

By the time we turned off the highway and onto our road, it was almost dark. Since there are hardly any houses nearby, there's almost no traffic. Just before we reached Home Sweet Home, Dad turned off our headlights.

"Spooky, isn't it?" Although we were still sitting in Purple Jeep, Mom talked softly.

I looked up at the turret. I'll admit, I didn't see a ghost. But in the moonlight, our house looked haunted anyway.

"Maybe this isn't such a good idea," Jason said.

"Not afraid, are you?" Mom asked.

"Of course not," my brother said. "There's probably nothing there."

"Anyhow, we've probably got the ghosts outnumbered," Dad said. "Let's go."

As usual, I was last in line. Ahead of me, my family walked single-file with flashlights ablaze.

My father's gigantic shape comforted me somewhat. In spite of his size, Dad's silhouette seemed to be almost gliding along through the weeds.

Behind him, my pregnant mother's shadow did what I call her *duck waddle.* I grinned. It was hard to believe that Mom, at this point, was actually hunting ghosts!

My brother's walk seemed nervous. Or maybe it was just the way Jason kept flashing his light from one side to the other.

As we all regrouped on the back stairs, I suddenly had an almost uncontrollable desire to laugh. I hoped Mom didn't feel the same way. If *she* ever got started, the whole adventure would be gone!

But Mom didn't laugh. In fact, nobody said a word. The only sound came from the field full of crickets.

Dad turned the key and pushed open the back door. It squeaked. He turned and whispered, "Someday I really must oil that hinge!"

We filed into the kitchen, and the door closed behind us. "So far, so good," Jason said. He flashed his light all around the room. Although everything was exactly the same as it had been a few hours before, in the dark everything looked different. Even my broom leaning in the corner cast a scary shadow.

"Be absolutely quiet," Mom whispered. "And let's stick together!"

Just as we were starting into the dining room, we heard a groan. Everybody froze. But we didn't hear the sound again.

"Old houses settle," Dad whispered. "The boards creak."

"I don't like it," Jason said.

We eased our way slowly into the dining room. "Oh, look!" Mom whispered. "The fireplace even looks good at night!"

"This isn't a house tour," Dad whispered. "We're hunting ghosts, remember!"

"Sorry," Mom giggled. She waddled over to the fireplace and shined her light up the chimney. "OK here," she said. "No ghosts of Christmas past!"

"Everybody try to be quiet," Dad said. "Let's go into the hall."

Nobody spoke. We shuffled along together.

"Are we going upstairs?" I asked.

"Of course," Mom said. "All the way up to the turret, if we have to."

I shivered.

"I forgot to tell you, Elizabeth," Dad whispered, "the boys got the living room all cleared out today."

"Really!" Mom shone her light into the back room. Suddenly the light stopped. It was shining on a bicycle.

"Do you see what I see?" Mom said.

"It looks like my bike," Jason whispered. "Shall I check it out?"

The rest of us watched while my brother tiptoed into the living room. He turned around and nodded his head. Then he came back into the hall. "What in the world?" he whispered. "How could my bike get in here?"

"Only one way," Dad said. "Robert must be

here in the house!"

"What would he be doing here tonight?" Jason asked.

"Let's find out!" Dad whispered.

Although we still were trying to be quiet, it seemed like the stairs creaked constantly as the four of us climbed to the second floor.

"Wait here," Dad said. With his light flashing along the floor ahead of him, he glanced into each of the four bedrooms. Nothing. Or, maybe I should say, *Nobody!*

Dad eased open the door to the third floor. "Robert!" he called softly. "Robert! Are you up there? It's Steve Hooper!"

We stood and waited.

"Robert?" Dad's voice sounded hollow.

"We're coming up!" Dad turned and motioned to us to follow him.

"Is Robert the ghost?" I asked. But nobody answered.

When we looked into the turret, we saw Robert. He was sitting on the floor among food wrappers. Under the windows was an opened sleeping bag.

"Don't shine your lights in his face," Dad told us. "Robert, what are you doing here? How did you get in the house?"

Robert rose to his feet. "It wasn't hard, Sir," he said. "I got in through the window and opened

119

the kitchen door from the inside. I didn't want Jason's bike to get stolen!"

"You've been staying here for several nights, haven't you?" Dad asked.

Robert nodded. "I didn't figure it would hurt anything. Actually, it was perfect. Every evening I rode into town to get food."

"But what about your friends in town?" Mom asked.

Robert shook his head. "I don't really know anybody in Woodland Park."

"Then what are you doing around here anyway?" Dad asked. "Where are you from? I think you owe us an explanation."

"I'm sorry I deceived you, Sir," Robert said. "My name is Robert Goff, and I'm from Denver. My father really does fix up old houses."

"Go on," Dad said.

"Maybe I wasn't thinking right. I don't know. I'm really confused. The problem is that my father's getting married again. See, Dad and I have been alone since Mom died. Just the two of us. Now I figure I'll just be in the way."

"Does your father know where you are?" Jason asked.

Robert shook his head again. "I had some money saved, so I just took off."

"You ran away?" I asked.

"I guess you could call it that," Robert said. "I

thought of it more like a vacation or something. But my money didn't last. Actually, this set-up here would have been perfect—except for that red-headed kid looking up and seeing me!"

"Then you really are the ghost!" I said.

Robert smiled at me. "I saw her looking up here, so I waved my arms. Her imagination did the rest!"

"I think you'd better come home with us, Robert," Mom said. "You can tell us more about it in the car."

"You know we'll have to contact your father," Dad said. "Or else the police."

"In the morning," Mom said.

"I can't believe it," Robert said. "You'd let me stay with you after what I've done?"

"You're hardly a stranger, Robert," Dad said. "You've been practically a member of the Hooper family for several days."

"How long have you been gone from home?" Mom asked.

"Nearly a week," Robert said. He knelt down and started rolling up his sleeping bag.

"Your father must be very worried," Dad said.

"I doubt it," Robert said. "My father has Michelle now. He doesn't need me anymore!"

Suddenly, without warning, Robert began to sob. He must have felt awful. I've never seen anyone cry so hard.

121

Robert's Family Reunion

Last night, Robert put his sleeping bag in Jason's room, which is across from mine in the loft. When I woke up this morning, I could hear the murmur of their voices. It turned out they had been talking for two hours.

I had prayed for Robert before I went to bed, and he was still on my mind this morning. I closed my eyes. "Dear Lord," I prayed, "did you wake them up? Please help Jason know what to say. I think Robert will listen to him. And please help everything to work out OK for Robert. Amen."

While I got dressed, I smiled. I realized that Robert was the first ghost I had ever prayed for!

As I slipped past my brother's room, I could

hear Jason talking. "I'm sorry your mother died," he said. "I don't know why it happened. But I do know you don't have to keep feeling all alone. Robert, Jesus loves you and He wants to comfort you."

When I got downstairs, Mom and Dad were in the kitchen. "I wish I could have talked to Robert's father," Dad said. "I always feel so stupid when I have to leave a message on an answering machine."

"I'm sure he'll be relieved to hear his son is all right," Mom said. "I hope he can get to the Woodland Park house before we have to leave tonight. It's so much closer and easier to find than the cabin."

Dad looked up. "Hi, Katie!" He gave me a hug. "Ready for some breakfast?"

"Steve, would you call the boys?" Mom asked.

After breakfast, everybody piled into Purple Jeep for the ride to Home Sweet Home. I sat in the back with Jason and Robert.

"Your family is really different," Robert said. "I've been noticing it all week."

"What do you mean?" Jason asked.

Robert paused. "It's hard to put into words. But you don't fight. And you all work together. It's like you're all on the same team!"

"Really!" I said. "You noticed that!"

"You seem surprised, Katie," Robert said.

"I guess we take our family for granted," Jason said. "We think all families are the same."

"They aren't," Robert said. "Take it from me. Oh, sometimes people put on an act in front of others! But you really seem to love each other. I've been thinking how lucky your baby will be!"

When we got to the house, it dawned on me that our mystery had been solved. Home Sweet Home isn't haunted any more! I couldn't wait to tell Sara.

"Can I work out in the yard so Sara can see me?" I asked.

Dad said I could. Then he turned to Robert and smiled. "Since this is probably your last day here, how do you think you can help us the most?"

Robert smiled back. "First, I'll work on security," he said. "From now on, nobody will enter this house unless he's invited!"

"Good!" Mom said. "I really don't think I'm up for any more late-night ghost hunting!"

Then Dad looked at Jason. "There's only one more room full of junk, Jason. How about if we clean that out together?"

Well, Sara didn't come over. As I finished another hour in the yard, my pile of trash was getting gigantic. And I started wondering if television could take up Sara's entire day.

Just as I was thinking about going in to talk

to Mom, a white truck pulled up in front of Purple Jeep. A man jumped out and ran toward me. "Is this where Steve Hooper lives?" he asked.

"We don't live here yet," I said. "But Steve Hooper's my father. He's working inside the house."

"Then I found the right place!" he said.

"You're Robert's father?" I asked.

The man nodded. "Where is my son?"

I took the man into the kitchen. "This is Robert's father," I told Mom.

Mr. Goff shook Mom's hand. "Bob Goff," he said. "I've come for my son."

Dad and Jason heard everybody talking and rushed into the kitchen. "Robert's upstairs," Dad said. "I'll get him."

But Mr. Goff couldn't wait. "This way?" he asked. And we heard him running upstairs.

Mom looked at Dad with tears in her eyes. "He must have left Denver as soon as he got your message," she said.

"He must love Robert very much!" Dad said.

Since Robert and his father didn't come right down, Mom suggested that we take a break and have lemonade on the back porch.

"It reminds me of the Bible story about the lost son," I said. "Only Robert didn't have to feed the pigs!"

"You mean the story in Luke 15," Dad said.

"That story shows us how much Jesus loves each person in the whole world. The Lord wants everyone to share in His love."

When Robert and Mr. Goff finally came down, it looked like they had both been crying.

"Robert's been telling me how he feels," Mr. Goff said. "I had no idea he felt that way."

"I hated to spoil your life," Robert said. "But I didn't want another mother."

"Nobody can take his mother's place," Mr. Goff said. "My wife was a very special person."

"Michelle's so different," Robert said. "She's nothing like Mom."

Mr. Goff nodded. "That's true. But during this past year, Michelle and I have gradually come to love each other." He put his arm around Robert's shoulder. "She wants to try to make a home for both of us."

"Dad told me upstairs that he still needs me," Robert said. "And I told him I'm ready to give Michelle a chance."

Mom smiled at Robert. "We'll pray for you, Robert," Mom said. "Personally, I think anyone would be proud to have you for a son!"

"Thanks, Ma'am."

"You know, you've been like my brother this week," Jason said. "I'll miss you!"

"And I'll never forget you!" Robert said. "Maybe you can come to visit me sometime."

126

"I'd like that," Jason said.

Dad smiled at Mr. Goff. "Before you leave, would you like a tour of our house? We couldn't have made such progress without Robert's help!"

"I'd love a tour," Mr. Goff said. "I don't know if Robert told you or not, but I do a lot of work with older houses."

They started walking around the first floor. And all of us tagged along.

"We just found this fireplace," Mom told him. "Believe it or not, it was covered with plaster-board!"

"That happens a lot," Mr. Goff said.

When we got to the hallway, Robert's father spotted the beautiful staircase right away. "It's one of the nicest I've ever seen!" he said. And Mom couldn't have been happier.

Because the front room still has trash in it, we didn't walk in there. But all of us paraded into the large back living room. Although Jason's bicycle still sat in the middle of the room, nobody mentioned it.

Robert's father walked right past the bike and started tapping on the rear wall. He grinned at Mom. "Guess what?" he said. "I think we just might find another fireplace back here!"

"I can't believe it!" Mom said.

"Would you like some help taking this wall

down?" Mr. Goff asked.

"Are you kidding!" Mom said. "That would be wonderful!"

"Just let me get a few tools from my truck," he said.

"I'll help you, Dad," Robert said. They walked out together.

With Mr. Goff's equipment, and with everybody helping, the progress was fast. I had to laugh when I remembered Sara and me pecking away at the other wall with our little hammers!

"Look here," Mr. Goff said. "It's another beauty! I think that's solid oak trim!"

Mom was kind of dancing around while she watched the progress. "Oh, Steve, God is so good!" she said. Just watching her made the rest of us smile!

When the wall was down, Mr. Goff looked at his watch. "Robert and I really should get started. Otherwise, we'll hit heavy traffic. But I'm afraid we're leaving you with a real mess in here."

"Don't be silly," Dad said. "We can take it from here. Can I pay you for your help?"

"Absolutely not!" Mr. Goff said. "I'm the one who's indebted to you! I can never repay you for looking out for Robert! I hate to think what might have happened if he'd gotten in with someone else!"

"We're glad we were here," Mom said.

"I do have a favor to ask," Dad said. "Bob, if I get stuck on a problem here, can I call you for advice?"

"I'm as near as the telephone!" Mr. Goff said. "It would be an honor to have you call!"

"Goodbye, Mr. Hooper," Robert said. "Thank you for forgiving me, Sir. I'll never forget you!" He turned to Mom. "Mrs. Hooper, promise you'll let me know about the baby?"

"I promise," Mom smiled. She went over and hugged him.

"Goodbye, Katie," Robert said. "And tell your red-headed friend I said 'goodbye.'"

Robert turned to Jason. "I'll miss you, Brother!" he said. "You've given me lots to think about, Jason!"

We walked out to the truck with them and watched them drive off.

"I think the Lord sent Robert here," Jason said.

"I think you're right," Dad said. "Now, gang, let's clean up that mess!"

We Find "It"

And still Sara didn't come over. By mid-afternoon I decided that if she hadn't come when I was finished sweeping the big living room, I'd go out and try to find her.

Suddenly, I heard her yell. "Katie. Katie Hooper!"

Grinning, I started running through the house. "Katie! KAT—IE HOOOOOPER!"

"You'd better hurry," Dad laughed. "This is almost as bad as hearing January howl!"

What surprised me as much as anything was that Sara was kneeling in our yard with her arms wrapped around my dog.

"Katie!" she yelled. "He likes me! January *likes* me!"

It did seem to be true. Whenever she opened her mouth, January looked at her with this stupid expression on his face.

"He's lonely," I said. "We haven't paid any attention to him all week. He's probably tired of guarding that boring dumpster."

"Give me some credit!" Sara said.

"I'm sorry," I told her. "Sara, I've missed you! Really I have."

"But I'm still not going in there," Sara said, as she glanced at Home Sweet Home.

"That's what I've been wanting to tell you. The ghost is gone. It was Robert. And he said to tell you goodbye."

"Details!" Sara said. "After all I've gone through, you'd better tell me more than that!" So we sat down on the back steps, and I filled her in on everything that had happened.

"I missed it," Sara said. "I missed the entire episode."

"I'm sorry," I said. "Even if you had been here, you were too afraid to come in the house."

Sara just looked at me. "You know, that's probably true. But I've got dibs on finding the secret treasure."

"Then you'll come in?"

She stood up. "What are we waiting for? Let's go!"

All this time, January stuck close to Sara. She

131

was petting him, and he was loving it. Even though I probably haven't played with him for a week, I still felt kind of jealous. Now, when we went inside, the dog came, too.

"Congratulations, Mrs. Hooper!" Sara said. "Where did you get all your courage?"

Mom laughed. "I'm not sure, Sara. I guess I just like adventures so much I don't think about being scared."

"And Robert's really gone?" Sara asked.

"He's really gone. But did Katie tell you his father discovered another fireplace?" Mom led the way into the living room. She looks at the fireplace every chance she gets.

"It's different from the other one," Sara said. "What's this little door for?"

"It's a wood box," Mom said, pulling it open. "You know, a place to keep logs."

When Mom left, Sara smiled and picked up the extra broom. I smiled, too. It seemed so natural to be sweeping with Sara. I felt sorry for Jason. He's really going to miss Robert! "This is the spot where Robert had parked Jason's bike," I remembered. "That's how Dad knew he was here."

"You could park a fleet of cars in here now," Sara said. "I hope you have lots of furniture."

"You'll see," I told her. "When Mom gets through with this house, it will be wonderful."

That's when Sara started looking around. She glanced into the hall. "I don't see January," she said. "Did he go with your mother?"

"Probably," I said.

When we finished sweeping, we stuck our brooms in the corner and headed for the kitchen. But Mom hadn't seen the dog. Neither had Jason and Dad. "Maybe January's upstairs looking for a ghost," Dad teased.

But January wasn't upstairs either. We even went up into the turret. Sara wanted to see exactly where Robert was sitting. Then she stood on tiptoes in front of the tower window. She waved her arms above her head and moaned, "OOOOOOOOooooooooo!"

"I guess from down there you couldn't tell it was Robert," I said.

"You'd better believe I couldn't!" she said.

"Are you thirsty? I think Mom still has some lemonade."

"Sounds good."

But we still didn't see January. He wasn't in the house, and he wasn't in the yard.

"Maybe he ran away!" Sara said. "He probably needs more love."

"Don't be silly," I said. "Maybe he's sleeping in Purple Jeep." But he wasn't.

"He's *gone!*" Sara said. "January's gone!"

"Where did you last see him?" Mom asked. It

was hard to remember. But we decided it was the living room, so we headed back in there. We no sooner walked into the room when we heard a familiar sound.

AaaOoooooo!

Sara and I looked at each other and grinned. The problem was that January sounded far away. But when we looked, we couldn't see him anywhere. *AaaOoooooo!*

The sound was clearest in the living room. But the room was empty. Except for the fireplace. "Sara," I said, "January must be in the wood-box."

We knelt down and looked in. It was dark. We didn't see the dog.

"I'll get a flashlight!" I said. "I think there's room for me to climb in."

With the light in my left hand, I crawled through the opening. What I discovered was another small closet behind the fireplace. And on the right was a narrow stairway! I stood up.

"Wait 'til you see this, Sara!" I called. "It's another secret passage. Come on in! There's room for both of us."

"I think I'm getting scared," Sara said.

"You'll miss out on the adventure!" I said. Well, the truth was that I didn't feel all that brave myself. But I held the light while Sara crawled through.

"Wow!" Sara said. She watched while I flashed my light up a brick wall behind the fireplace. Then I flashed it up the narrow stairs.

Near the top of the little stairway, moaning softly, sat January. He looked scared.

"I'm going up after him," I said. "Will you be OK waiting here in the dark?" If Sara started to scream again, there was no telling what might happen.

"I'll be OK," she said. "In my whole life I may never get another chance for an adventure!"

January was huddled on the top step. He was trembling when I put my arms around him. "It's OK, really it is," I told him.

"Is he all right?" Sara called.

"I think he's just scared," I said.

"What's up there?"

"Nothing," I said. "The stairs just stop!"

Since January's too heavy to carry, I took hold of his collar in my right hand and started down. With the flashlight in my left hand, I couldn't hang on to the wall. It took us a long time to get to the bottom.

"Sara, you were very brave, waiting here in the dark," I said.

Sara smiled a weak little smile. "This is kind of neat in here, isn't it! Do you suppose this could be where the treasure's hidden?"

"I think it's our best possibility," I said. "But

with January in here, we can't really look. Maybe we could push him back out into the living room."

"Where's the door?" Sara asked. Her voice showed signs of panic.

"Right there," I said. I flashed my light down. "Just push on it."

We finally shoved January through the door. "I hope he doesn't start howling," Sara said. We waited and listened. Fortunately, January didn't howl. All we heard was an occasional moan. "Poor thing," Sara said.

"It's just for a little while," I told her. "If Jason gets here first, we'll never find the treasure."

I flashed my light up and down the wall of bricks. They all looked exactly alike. Except for one. It stuck out funny. "Look, Sara," I said. "Do you see anything different about that brick? The one toward the left?"

"Which one?" While I held the light, Sara ran her hands along the wall. Suddenly, as she touched the funny-looking brick, it moved. And there, built into the brick wall behind the fireplace, was a drawer!"

I was so excited I nearly dropped the flashlight.

Sara pulled open the drawer, and we saw a slim metal box. "Katie, we found it!" she yelled. "We found the secret treasure!"

We Share Our Secrets

I held the flashlight while Sara lifted the box from the drawer. "I can't wait!" I said. "Hurry! Open it!"

"I'm trying," Sara said. "Maybe I can get a better grip on it if I push the drawer back in."

"Want me to do it?"

"I said I'm trying!" Sara said. "Hold the light steady."

But it was no use. Sara couldn't get the lid off. And then she took a turn holding the light, but I couldn't get it off either.

"What can we do?" she asked.

And then we heard voices. "Katie! Sara! Where are you?" Mom called.

We looked at each other. "No matter what happens, it's still our treasure," Sara said. "We'll always be the ones who found it."

"For now, let's stick it back," I said.

As we shoved open the little door, January started howling. *AaaaaOoooo!* By the time we crawled through the opening, my whole family was standing in the living room watching.

"What's happening?" Jason asked.

"You were right," I told my brother. "There is another secret passage! January found it!"

"All right!" Jason didn't think he needed an invitation. He headed right for the door we had just come out of. Naturally, Sara and I went back in after him.

"It just stops," I said, as we flashed my light up the stairs. "I've already been up there."

But Jason had to see for himself. "It has to lead somewhere," he told us. That's why I had to stand at the bottom in the dark with Sara. We watched him climb to the top of the stairs and back down again. It seemed like forever.

"I think I have it figured out," Jason said. "I'll bet the two passages used to be connected! Isn't the upstairs closet right above this fireplace?"

"Of course," I said. "And that's why I could hear you and Robert talking when I was sweeping up in that bedroom!"

"How come we can't get through?" Sara asked.

"Somebody must have put up a wall," Jason

138

said. "It could be like the ones that closed off the two fireplaces."

"Let's tell Mom and Dad!" I said. They were waiting for us. Besides, the space behind the fireplace really was too small for all of us!

Of course, Mom was thrilled! "I'd love to see the passageway!" she said.

I looked at her. "I think you'll have to wait until after the baby is born," I said. "You'd never fit now!"

Dad has a good sense of humor about his size. "Then I guess I might never get to see it!" he laughed. "Maybe you can take pictures!"

Mom smiled. "Well, this sure has been an exciting day, all right!"

Sara and I looked at each other. "There's something else!" I said. "You tell them, Sara!"

"Way before you got here, I heard there was a secret treasure in this house," Sara said. She paused dramatically. "We think we found it!"

"What did you find?" Dad asked.

"Where is it?" Mom wondered.

"In a box," I said. I told them about the loose brick and the secret drawer behind the fireplace.

"Let's go!" Jason exclaimed.

"Let us go first," I said. "After all, we found it!" We all crawled back through the door.

I was the one that carried the box out into the

living room. "We couldn't get it open," I explained.

"Let's have a look," Dad said. As it turned out, he had to send Jason to get his screwdriver.

And all the time we waited, the suspense was building up.

Finally, Dad got the lid loose. "OK, girls," he smiled, "it's all yours!"

We lifted the lid and stared inside the box. We saw gold! There were shiny gold nuggets, all right. But they were stuck into something white.

"Gross!" Sara said. "Those white things look like *teeth!*"

"They *are* teeth," I said. I can't tell you how disappointed I felt! "Why would anyone collect teeth?"

"Maybe the house belonged to the tooth fairy," Dad laughed.

"Maybe it used to belong to a dentist," Mom said.

"I think those wires do look exactly like real gold!" Jason said.

"And the flat pieces of paper in that bottle look like gold leaf," Dad added. He looked up at us. "You know, this gold could be valuable! I don't know the current price, but these days just an ounce of pure gold is worth hundreds of dollars!"

"Wow!" Sara said, "Did you hear that!"

"You know," I said, "I just thought of something. I think Home Sweet Home probably *did* belong to a dentist! I never told you, but Sara and I found clues in an upstairs closet. There are lots of postcards addressed to Dr. Willard. Only I thought that Dr. Willard was a doctor!"

"Dr. Willard may have had his practice right here in this house," Mom said. "Lots of dentists used to do that."

"It makes sense," Dad agreed. "A dentist would have kept gold around to make crowns. It's stronger than silver."

Sara looked amazed. "Then you mean we really did find a treasure?"

"It looks that way!" Dad said.

Sara started dancing around. I joined her. Then Mom joined both of us.

"Hey," Dad laughed. "I hate to break this up, but it's getting late. We'd better get started for the cabin!"

"Steve, I think this calls for a celebration!" Mom said. "I have an idea. Let's eat supper in Woodland Park!" We were so surprised that at first everybody just looked at her.

"Can Sara come, too?" I asked. "After all, half the treasure belongs to Sara!"

"We'd love for you to join us, Sara!" Dad said. "But you'll have to ask your parents."

141

"Sure," Sara agreed. "I'll leave a note for my mother."

While Sara ran home, the rest of us made sure everything at Home Sweet Home was locked up tight. And then we watched while Dad pulled the kitchen door shut and locked it. Naturally, as always, the door squeaked.

"I have an idea," Mom said. "Let's not oil that hinge, Steve. Then whenever we hear that door squeak, we'll remember our ghost!"

"And our secret passages!" Jason said.

"And our treasure!" I added. "We can't forget the secret treasure!"

Dad nodded and put the key back in his pocket. And then all of us, including January, climbed into Purple Jeep to wait for Sara.